Girls in Charge

Also by Debra Moffitt

Only Girls Allowed
Best Kept Secret
The Forever Crush

Girls in Charge

THE PINK LOCKER SOCIETY

Debra Moffitt

ST. MARTIN'S GRIFFIN

NEW YORK

This is a work of fiction. All of the characters, organizations, and events portrayed in this novel are either products of the author's imagination or are used fictitiously.

www.stmartins.com

ISBN 978-0-312-64506-9

First Edition: September 2011

Printed in August 2011 in the United States of America by RR Donnelley, Harrisonburg, Virginia

10 9 8 7 6 5 4 3 2 1

Girls in Charge

One

Valentine's Day should be outlawed. Really. I was just getting used to being Forrest's former fake girlfriend, when it popped up on the calendar like a dentist appointment. The Valentine's Day carnation sale at my school didn't help one bit. This annual fund-raiser, organized by the seventh-graders, helped pay for the eighth-grade spring trip. The flower sale involved buckets of white, pink, and red carnations that could be purchased and delivered to the person of your choice. With a note.

For just a dollar, you could remind your best friend that you adore her, tell your track coach that she's awesome, or toss a romantic volley at someone you think is super-cute, funny, and wonderful.

But don't worry—I did *not* send Forrest a red carnation. Or a pink one or a white one. I sent him nothing, did nothing of any sort to mark this day of chubby cherubs, candy hearts, and love.

But I did *receive* a carnation—a pink one—from someone who decided not to send any note. Or maybe the note fell off. But either way, at lunch on Valentine's Day, my biggest fear was relieved when I received my note-less carnation. You don't want people thinking no one cares enough to send you at least one.

That's kind of why I sent a pink carnation to Mimi Caritas, Clem's sixth-grade sister. Clem is a real-deal teen model and Mimi is just an ordinary girl who's a little afraid to grow up. She's actually an ordinary girl who until a few months ago hated the PLS and tried to put us out of business. But it's all been worked out and I feel like she needs a big sister who's a little nicer and a little less stunningly beautiful.

I held my breath when the vice president of the seventh-grade class approached our cafeteria table. For a long moment, the always friendly Shannon Andersen stood there, studying her order sheet, with that white plastic bucket of tall carnations sloshing in water.

Then she reached into her bucket and pulled out a small bunch for Kate—one from me, of course. Shannon reached back in and pulled out a whole bouquet for Piper. Seriously, a committee of boys seems to pursue her at all times. Then it was my turn. I received three—a white one from my friend Bet, a white one from Kate and Piper, and the anonymous pink one.

"Where's the card?" I asked Shannon.

All the other carnations had small, pink construction paper cards attached to them by a loop of red yarn.

"No clue," she said.

I stopped her before she moved on to the next table.

"But isn't there some kind of master list or something?" I asked.

Then I grabbed the edge of her bucket and peered in to see if there were any notes left floating in there.

"Um, we're not that organized," Shannon said, smiling at me but also pulling back on her bucket. "You should see the Art room where we're putting all these deliveries together."

I let her go and started to run through all the possible explanations for the pink carnation I was holding. More than likely it was Jake Austin, who I knew liked me. There's nothing wrong with Jake. I even danced with him at the Backward Dance. But there was also nothing particularly right about Jake. He was a just a nice guy—a friend—who didn't give me butterflies in my stomach.

My stomach lurched, however, at the thought that

Forrest's younger brother, Trevor, might have sent the carnation. After I left a note for Forrest that was accidentally intercepted by his sixth-grade brother, Trevor *still* winks at me in the hallway. When you're in eighth grade, on your way to high school, you do not want to be known as the girl who crushes on a sixth-grade boy. Trevor never quite got the message and gives me the winky-wink every time we cross paths.

For all my questions about this pink flower, one thing seemed sure: Forrest had nothing to do with it. We had remained "friends" following my decision to break off our fake relationship. For us, "friends" meant the occasional hi and not much else. Just the other day, I saw him and his old girlfriend, Taylor Mayweather, standing together at his locker. She looked like she was crying and he was leaning down, trying to get her to look at him. What do I make of that? Nothing good, I'm sure. If Forrest sent anyone a carnation this year, I bet it was her.

"I need to find a vase for these," Piper said dramatically. She pronounced "vase" as *vahz*, and I feared she would slip into French as she'd been doing lately. When Shannon gave her the flower, she exclaimed, "*Merci, mademoiselle!*" (Thank you, miss!)

Piper held her flowers upright, as if they were in an imaginary *vahz*. Then she arranged them in a professional-looking way, as I'd seen her mother do.

Kate laughed as Piper hurried off, then she turned her attention to me. She knew what I was thinking about. Petal by petal, I was putting together the clues surrounding my mysterious pink flower.

Two

By day's end, I could see that some people's carnations were already going limp. So I was careful to protect mine on the bus ride home. In my room, I put the two white flowers on my desk in a skinny vase. The single pink carnation went into a tall, blue plastic bottle I found in our recycling bin. I was careful to give it just the right amount of cold water. I set it on my nightstand. Then, silently, I said something that had become sort of a little prayer:

I will not waste time thinking about Forrest. I will focus on:

1. *being a good friend*
2. *becoming a better runner*

3. *school*
4. *learning how to be a big sister (Mom's expecting!)*
5. *giving good advice on the Pink Locker Society Web site*

Silly as it might have been, I had a personal mission statement now. We had a goal-setting class once, where the teacher said everyone should have one. It sounded weird to me at the time, but now it made more sense. I even made myself a soda tab bracelet to remind me of the five parts. It was five soda tabs threaded on a pink ribbon. I used four silver and one that I painted with pink nail polish in honor of the Pink Locker Society.

I also found a way to give myself credit for keeping on track with my five goals. I started out the day with my bracelet on my right wrist. If I made it through a whole day without thinking of Forrest, it remained on my right wrist. If I didn't, I moved the bracelet to the left wrist. At first, I had plenty of left-wristed days. But I was slowly learning how to forget him.

It was easy to be busy. Track team practices were starting, my mom was getting ready to have a baby (in June!), and the Pink Locker Society was moving in a new and exciting (and possibly terrifying) direction. First off, we were actually moving. Thanks to Mrs. Percy and our reunion with her sister, Edith, we were taking up residence again in the posh office behind our pink locker doors. No more basement meetings! We couldn't wait to once again gather around our glass conference table. We longed to update the Pink Locker Web site from our comfy office as we sipped iced tea from our fridge.

We answered tons of questions about girls' feelings about their bodies and everyone's fear of being embarrassed. There were so many ways to embarrass yourself. Maybe your mom won't let you shave your hairy legs. Or you don't have a bra and everyone else does. Or everyone is always talking about their periods, and you don't have yours yet.

That was me—thirteen and no period. But after answering hundreds of questions about periods, I knew that they come on their own schedule. A girl could be as young as nine or as old as me. So I felt better knowing I was normal but I really did hope that my period would happen soon. I mean, it seemed like something you should have over with before you go to high school, right? Well, high school would be starting for me in the fall.

So I was still waiting, but the whole experience of waiting had given me a brilliant idea. What if we could predict when someone was going to get her period? I mean, isn't that the question every middle-school girl wants to know? Yes, they're tricky, but periods don't just come like lightning bolts out of the blue. There are stages, you know, steps along the way. For instance, girls develop breasts first, then comes the period about two years or so later. And there were other signs, too, which I knew from talking to the school nurse and my own doctor. Why couldn't the Pink Locker Society create a kind of Magic 8 Ball for girls?

So my mind was whirring with plans for the PLS, but I was also a little worried. Here was the part that had my nerves jangling: Mrs. Percy, Edith, and even Ms. Russo wanted us to go public.

"Don't you believe in girl power?" Mrs. Percy had asked me.

Yes, of course. But also no. Here's why: We could get into big trouble here. The principal had *visited my house* and told all our parents about the Pink Locker Society. Then he said we needed to stop immediately. So by going public with the PLS, we'd be saying, "Hey, we ignored you and we're going to keep on ignoring you." Not to mention my parents. I hadn't told them we had restarted PLS, either.

"It's ultimately your decision," Ms. Russo had advised. "But I think it's the right path."

Three

Re-entry day was like going back in time. Sure, our original entry through the pink locker doors had been just six months before. But so much had happened, with all those basement meetings in between. I felt like a different person. But not so different that I didn't stress about whether I'd be able to open the weird combination lock that had letters instead of numbers. At least the new combination was easy: P-I-N-K.

The hour of study hall came and I fiddled in my locker for a bit, wasting time and waiting for everyone to clear out. I watched Forrest out of the corner of my eye as he dropped off his stuff and left for the gym. I had this weird feeling that he was doing the same thing, and sneaking a peek at me. But then I realized that was probably too good to be true.

With my right hand, I twisted my dial to the P, to the I, to the N, and to the K. The mechanical *thunk* told me I'd done it right on the first try. I opened the pink locker door just slightly. Then I closed my real locker door, with me inside it like a magician's assistant about to disappear. I opened the pink door and stepped down onto the plush carpeting. Inside, our office was well lit, cozy yet professional. A real-looking office, where real work would be done. No more sitting on jumbo packages of paper towels in the dingy school basement.

There was a huge arrangement of green ivy and baby pink roses in the center of our conference table. It was so big we had to move it in order to see each other as Kate, Piper, and I gathered around. Piper brought the pink laptop and it started to hum to life. Did you ever just feel like you were in the right place at exactly the right time? That's how I felt at that moment, at that table, with my two best friends. I wouldn't have been surprised if I had held out my hand and a warm cup of tea landed on it.

Of course, that didn't happen. But it did seem magical that someone had fixed us a pot of tea. Our fairy godmothers (aka Mrs. Percy, Ms. Russo, and Edith) had also set out three china teacups on saucers along with some kind of cinnamon strudel bread.

Kate poured the tea and I started talking about my plan for the Magic 8 Ball Period Predictor. A girl could answer some questions about herself, her age, and physical changes she had experienced so far. Then, using a bit of computer code, we could compute an estimate of when she'd get her period. How perfect would this be! No more worrying it would happen at some unfortunate time—like at school or on the first day of a beach vacation.

"Are you sure, Jemma?" Piper asked.

"Yeah, these things are pretty unpredictable," Kate said. She gave me a knowing look. She was the only one who knew I wasn't in the period club yet. Piper assumed I was and I never corrected her.

"I disagree," I said. "Periods are predictable if you know certain things about puberty and what happens first, second, and third."

"And that's something you know now?" Piper asked.

I explained how the medical books say a girl's period usually comes two to two and a half years after she starts developing breasts.

"Therefore, we ask girls on what day they got their

first bra and add two to two and a half years to that," I said.

"I have to say it would relieve a lot of worry and confusion," Kate said.

Questions about first periods accounted for approximately twenty percent of all questions submitted to the Pink Locker Society. In other words, one out of every five questions was about this subject, I said.

Kate raised her eyebrows, impressed.

"It could potentially cut down on our workload," I said.

We had made good on our goal of answering five questions a week, but we were buried in more questions than we would ever have a chance of answering.

"Yes, let's try it," Piper said. "Why not?"

What I didn't reveal was that I had already done this calculation for myself. The Period Predictor said I would get my period no later than March 21—just three weeks away.

Four

There's something weird about your mom being pregnant. Of course, you can guess the obvious, non-weird parts. You spend lots of time thinking about your new brother or sister. We were planning a baby shower, for example. The name game can eat up an evening. And we'd chosen a new color for the guest bedroom, which would become the baby's room. It was yellow, owing to my parents' refusal to find out if we were having a boy or a girl.

"Let's cherish the pleasant surprise," my mom explained when I asked—no, begged—that they find out already. Now for the weird part. I worry about my mom and the baby and that everything will turn out all right. I mean, Mom will be going to the hospital and everyone knows it's hard work to have a baby. I don't want her to be in any pain. Would they want me in the delivery room? Wow, I hope not.

I also worried (a little) about how things would change when the baby comes. I wasn't talking about the diapers and the crying, which everyone jokes about. I was thinking about our day-to-day world. It had been just the three of us since . . . well, since forever!

From the topic of my particular little family, it's not much of a leap to think about the future day when I might get married and, eventually, have a baby of my own. It feels as far as Mars from me right now. And boys might as well be Martians because I don't understand a thing about them, even though I spent seventy-one days as Forrest McCann's pretend girl-friend.

Yes, he put his arm around me and kissed me. We even talked about real-life stuff. But I remember him saying, "Girls always want answers, Jem. I don't have any answers." He told me even he didn't know how he felt or why he did the things he did. So if that's the case, how could I ever understand him?

Stop, stop, stop. You don't want to move that bracelet today.

I looked down at my soda tabs that reminded me of my five goals. Big sisterhood, school, friends, the PLS, and running.

Did I mention I'm on the cross-country team for real this year? And now that spring is on the way, practices have begun. I'm not super-fast yet. I've run in a few 5Ks, which are about three miles. But the truth is I wasn't prepared for the hills and I needed to stop and walk. I do not want to do that in a real cross-country race. When I run in a race, I'm thinking about looking silly and not finishing and everyone who's passing me.

But when I'm just running, no pressure, my mind just clears, like clouds lifting. My thoughts go to a new place and I sometimes figure out what I'm going to do about this or that. I get in a rhythm and my brain goes somewhere that I can't get to otherwise, even in a quiet room all alone. It could be the sweating or the measured puffs of breath. Or maybe it's the steady beat of my feet as they hit the ground. I'm never really running away from anything. But what I'm running toward I don't exactly know.

Five

We all jumped out of our cushy office chairs when the phone rang. Kate answered and we all watched her as she talked.

"It's Ms. Russo," she said, and pressed the speaker-phone button.

"And Edith," another voice chimed in. "It's no secret that you girls will be graduating eighth grade before you know it. Where did the time go?"

"And what have you decided about going public with the PLS?" Ms. Russo asked.

We hadn't decided anything as far as I was concerned.

"I agree that the secrecy thing just takes up a lot of time," Piper said. "Let's get it out in the open."

Kate nodded her agreement.

"I agree," she said.

"Excellent," Ms. Russo said.

Then Kate and Piper both turned to me, warily. I was clearly the holdout here.

"We haven't heard from Jemma on the question, have we?" Edith asked.

"I-I don't think it's excellent," I said. "Won't we get in trouble, like instantly?"

"We're going to see to it that you don't," Edith said.

"That would be awesome," Piper said. "Then our work is done here. Or not done. You know what I mean."

"How are you going to see to it that we don't get suspended or worse?" I asked.

Both Ms. Russo and Edith let a few beats pass before answering, which made me even more concerned.

"We have people on the inside, as you know," Edith finally said.

"And I have every confidence that that particular person will be very effective," Ms. Russo said.

I knew who they meant and mouthed "Mrs. Percy" to Kate and Piper.

"People do say she pretty much runs the school," Piper said.

"She's impressive in her influence, to be sure," Edith said.

"Can you guarantee us that she will smooth things over with Principal F. so that nothing happens to us? That's what I'm looking for," I said.

"Ah, youth," Edith said. "I wish I could give you a gold-standard guarantee, but I can't. What I can say is that it feels like a risk worth taking."

"Think of the brave women who've come before you. No one just handed women the right to vote, remember?" Ms. Russo said.

Oh, great. Now she's comparing us to Susan B. Anthony.

"I'm up for an adventure," Piper said.

"And I think, you know, it will all work out," Kate said. She looked at me, since I was the only one who needed convincing.

I felt surrounded and I gave in by simply lifting my palms skyward as if to say "I have no argument left." Well, I did have one argument but I wasn't going to share it since it was, simply "I'm chicken."

Ms. Russo explained that they'd planned a meeting with Principal Finklestein to discuss the matter. They'd bring along Mrs. Percy so she could push our case.

"I do wonder what he's going to say," Kate said.

But Kate said her worries had given way to her feeling that this was the right decision.

"We're doing something good here. Maybe not, like, heroic, but important at Margaret Simon Middle School," she said.

"Right-o," Edith said. "You girls should discuss how you'd like us to proceed."

"I think we should be at the meeting," Piper said.

"I agree one hundred percent," Ms. Russo said. "This is a girls' movement. You should do some of the talking."

Gulp. This is not what I'd imagined. Sitting in the principal's office and admitting that we'd been carrying on with the PLS all along, and that we now planned to reveal ourselves to the whole school?

Kate read the look on my face and suggested that just us girls talk and get back to the grown-ups about what to do next about the meeting.

"Great," Ms. Russo said. "Oh, and I have some exciting news. I've nominated you three to speak at the national Tomorrow's Leaders Today conference."

I had heard about this conference, but until now, I had known only total brainiacs to attend. You know, eighth-graders who already know which college they're going to and expect to be president of the United States someday.

"You're going to talk about the Pink Locker Society and how other girls can form a group like this at their school," Ms. Russo said.

"So it's already decided?" I asked.

"Well, the committee was very impressed when I described your work," Ms. Russo said. "There's even interest in having a session for boys. Wouldn't it be incredible to create Blue Locker Societies, too?"

"What about Principal F.?" I asked.

"By the time of the conference, the PLS will be out in the open, right?" Ms. Russo said.

By this point, Kate and I were speechless. But Piper leaned over the table, with interest, toward the speakerphone.

"Where is this conference?" she asked.

Ms. Russo answered with three of the most exciting words I'd ever heard.

New. York. City.

Of course we wanted to go, even if it meant we'd have to work on a session about Blue Locker Societies. Having the chance to stay in a hotel and explore the coolest city in the world was just too amazing to pass up.

Six

It was normal for my parents to know very little about what I was thinking. I mean, I was getting older and it was my life and all. But I was sort of reaching a point where there was too much they didn't know. I was constantly thinking about the Pink Locker Society and the New York City trip. None of us had told our parents we restarted the PLS, so we couldn't spill the beans yet about the trip. And, of course, our parents would have to say okay and sign the permission form. That meant the two topics that were most on my mind—that I'd most like to discuss—were completely unavailable for dinnertime discussion. When my parents asked, "What's new with you?" I froze.

I started to feel confined by how much they didn't know. And as plans unfolded for taking the Pink Locker Society public, it seemed high time to tell them.

I picked a time when I thought they'd be most understanding. It was Sunday afternoon and I had just folded a load of laundry. I delivered the items like a mailman to our bedrooms and other spots in the house as appropriate. I brought the empty basket downstairs to where they were sitting together, reading the Sunday paper and drinking coffee.

"Okay, I have something to say."

They both looked up. My dad peeked at me over the sports page.

"Well, remember the Pink Locker Society?"

They nodded and looked at each other.

"The Web site, the whole Principal Finklestein fiasco?" Dad asked.

Having the principal show up at your house after school was definitely quite a fiasco.

"Yeah, that's it. Well, it's still going," I said.

"Okay, and who's running it now?" Mom asked.

"I am," I answered hesitantly. "Me and Kate and Piper. And sometimes Bet."

My parents shared a look of surprise and then looked back at me.

"How long has this been going on?" Dad asked.

"Since not long after we were supposed to have shut it down. When we got the laptop back."

"I knew this would happen," Mom said, resting her folded newspaper on her belly. "You girls are going to be in a heap of trouble if the principal finds out."

"Susan B. Anthony got in a lot of trouble, too. And now she's a hero. She's on a coin, right?"

I was stammering here, making a comparison I didn't exactly buy myself.

"I'm not sure what Susan B. Anthony has to do with your particular situation," Mom said, narrowing her eyes.

"I have to agree it doesn't explain your being dishonest with us," Dad said.

I closed my eyes, praying that some kind of convincing explanation would come flying out of my mouth. To my shock, it did. It wasn't pure accident, though. I dug deep for the truest, true feeling I had about the whole situation.

"I'm proud of how we've helped girls," I said. "It's the only important thing I've really done in my whole life."

My parents both smiled at this, and I spotted the early signs of me winning them over. Then I told them how we answer questions from girls every week who have all sorts of problems.

"They are so happy we answer their questions even when we don't have easy answers, like when it's about bullying or someone's parents getting divorced," I continued.

"Where is all this going on?" my mother asked.

"In the school basement, in study hall."

"Is it safe down there?" my mother asked.

I thought about the dark, the dust, and the churning furnace, but told her it was fine.

"It's . . . noble, yes. Certainly sounds so, but I'm still not over your going against the explicit orders from Prinicpal Finklestein," Mom said.

Though I was still nervous myself, I explained how we were going public with help from Ms. Russo, Edith, and Mrs. Percy.

My mother, placing a hand on her belly, said that she couldn't argue against the Pink Locker Society.

"It's a good concept," she said. "I've never had a quarrel with that. Girls need help, and why not get it from other girls?"

But—and this was a pretty serious but—she and Dad wanted to talk with Ms. Russo. I know they wanted to see if my story checked out.

This was perfectly fine with me because then Ms. Russo could break the news to them about New York City. And once she did that, I could start talking nonstop about NYC and what we'd do there and where we'd stay and how we'd eat the best pizza on earth and see the city lights twinkle like diamonds as we trotted through Central Park by horse-drawn carriage.

Seven

Bet still had her weekly show on Margaret Simon Middle School TV. But it was not the hard-hitting kind of journalism she had in mind when she was awarded the honor in the fall. Principal Finklestein had had weekly flip-outs when her shows featured important topics like the Pink Locker Society and the fairness of the annual Backward Dance. So now we had been broadcasting Bet's real shows on the Pink Locker Society Web site, which allowed her to report on hard-hitting topics like bullying and the Fat or Not–list incident.

When it came to being on MSTV, Principal Finklestein had pretty much ordered Bet to stick to bland topics, such as study skills, lunch-table etiquette, and the history of the Margaret Simon Middle School flower garden. But she was awarded one big story: She got to announce the destination for this year's eighth-grade trip.

As the time of announcement neared, everyone was buzzing with guesses. Some were far-fetched like Hawaii or Antarctica. But we all really knew it would be somewhere that could be easily reached from where we lived. It couldn't be too far or too expensive, but previous classes had gone to lots of cool places, including Boston and Washington, D.C.

We grilled Bet at lunch on Friday, the day of her weekly broadcast, but she wouldn't give us even a hint.

"It's a city, is all I'll say," Bet said.

"Oh, thanks, that narrows it down," Piper said.

"You'll just have to wait," Bet said.

"What if we give you an even better story, will you tell us then?" Piper said.

I shot Piper a look that said "What are you doing?"

"Oh, come on, Jem. You know we're going to tell her anyway."

"It is a pretty good story," Kate said with a mischievous grin.

"Tell us, *s'il vous plaît*!" Piper pleaded *en Francais*.

"It has to do with your favorite person, Principal Finklestein," I said.

"And your real favorite people, us, the Pink Locker Society," Kate said.

"Okay. I'll give you a hint," Bet said. "New Amsterdam."

She ran off to prepare for the afternoon and her broadcast while the rest of us shook our heads. Did that mean we were going to New Amsterdam? Because none of us had ever heard of it.

That afternoon, during last period, the eighth grade was more polite than usual during Bet's broadcast. I mean, they paid more attention back when she did serious stuff. But these days, most people just talked or doodled during her shows. But the classroom was quiet, waiting for the news. Eighth-grade trips were legendary. Traveling together and staying overnight was just so grown-up, and the potential freedom—even with chaperones—was tantalizing.

Bet sat behind her anchor desk and spun a globe.

"Where will it be, eighth grade?"

"I'm crossing my fingers for Paris," Piper whispered to me.

We watched Bet halt the spinning Earth and the camera followed her finger to the east coast of the United States—no big surprise. Then the lens zeroed in to show that she was pointing at New York.

Cheers erupted in our classroom and could be heard echoing down the hall. People hugged and jumped up and down until Mr. Ford asked us to "kindly return to your seats." But even he high-fived a few of us and revealed he'd be going as a chaperone. I was thinking about the Tomorrow's Leaders Today conference. Did that mean I'd be going to New York City twice?

The rest of the class was buzzing noisily about their big-city plans when Mr. Ford approached my desk.

"You can thank Ms. Russo for that," he said confidentially.

"What?"

"Well, the class trip was supposed to be to Williamsburg, Virginia, but Jane found out it conflicted with your conference. She convinced the trip committee to go to New York instead. You'll be able to do both."

Eight

Some days, they shouldn't call it cross-country practice. They should call it a mud bath. That's what it was like to run in the wet, soppy springtime. It might have been sunny, but the hint of winter was still in the air. Wherever my sneaker landed, the ground was so wet I kicked up dots of mud on the back of my legs.

That doesn't sound fun, does it? Well, somehow it still managed to be fun for me. I was getting better at running. I wish I would have tallied up every mile since I started running. Had I run one hundred miles yet, I wondered? When would I run two hundred? Lots of girls say they can't run.

What they mean is that they can't run for very

long. But here's a secret. You *can* run. If I can run, you can run. You start small. You run for a little bit. You run around the block. You walk fast, then you run. And before you know it, it gets easier. You've run a mile and you're done. You didn't even have to stop.

If you're like me, you get to one mile and you don't want to stop. Now, by mile two, I wanted to stop, but even then, I tried to keep going. And I figured maybe someday, I'd be able to just keep going. A marathon is 26.2 miles. Something to shoot for.

So I kept going on that chilly March afternoon. *Splish-squelch.* I was deep in my running brain, thinking about nothing and everything all at once. Then I saw him: Forrest. Just up ahead, he was carrying his baseball bag and some bases. Baseball season was starting up, so of course I'd be seeing him out here occasionally. Did seeing him mean that I had let myself think about him and I had to switch my bracelet to the other wrist? I hoped not. And what if he stopped me, would that count? Because that is exactly what happened next.

"Hey, Jemma, hold up?"

I slowed to a trot and then walked the last few paces toward him. He was standing there in a hoodie. He dropped his stuff and waited for me. I didn't even have time to think of how I looked.

"I'm supposed to ask you about this New York thing. Ms. Russo wants me to do something with the Blue Locker Society, whatever that's supposed to be," he said.

"Oh? Nobody told me about that."

"Yeah, I guess we're supposed to talk or something. At some conference?" Forrest said.

"She wants you to talk to me? Um, okay. When?"

"Monday study hall, at the lockers," he said. He picked up his bag and hustled down the hill to the baseball diamond.

I watched him go all the way down the hill to the group of players warming up. I remembered Ms. Russo saying something about a Blue Locker Society, but how did Forrest get involved? What were the two of us supposed to discuss?

I was still so stunned it took me a moment to get running again. I knew I'd be calling Kate about this one. But my run wasn't over so it was just me, the mile ahead, and my thoughts. Enough time to make a decision. It would be all business when I met with Forrest.

Kate said the Blue Locker Society idea came up because the leaders' conference is co-ed—both girls and boys.

"And Ms. Russo thinks that it would be good for boys to have a Blue Locker Society," Kate said.

"They have just as many questions as girls, they just keep quiet about them," Ms. Russo had told Kate.

Mr. Ford asked for volunteers and Forrest was the only one who said he'd do it, Kate said.

"Uh, okay. I guess I get it."

Nine

So my Monday meeting with Forrest came and went and I stayed calm the entire time. I didn't wear anything special. I didn't write down what I would say. I just decided I'd answer his questions and be nice, but not flirty-friendly.

It was Forrest who seemed nervous. He was the first one at the lockers and we decided to go to the gym to talk. Otherwise, teachers would snag us for not having hall passes. I, for certain, didn't want to get caught. Technically, I had never been assigned a study hall room, so we could have our Pink Locker meetings. But today, Kate and Piper were meeting without me.

"What do you want to know?" I asked after we

settled into a spot on the bleachers. The gym was empty except for the sixth-grade square dance club.

"Do you remember when we did square dancing in sixth grade?" Forrest said.

I laughed out loud, thinking of that square dance music and all those unusual commands—do si do, allemande left.

"Deadly," Forrest said. "You have absolutely no control over who is your partner."

For a moment, I flashed to a time in sixth grade when we were square dance partners.

"But they look like they're having fun," I said.

The music stopped and the class was supposed to be realigning their squares. But some couples were swinging their partners, just for the fun of it. Mimi Caritas and her partner were among them.

"Okay, what do you need to know?" I said, turning to face him.

"Know?"

"About the Pink Locker Society or the Blue Locker Society, or whatever this is about."

"Are you mad?" he asked me.

"What would I be mad about? It's just that I don't really understand what all this is about."

I was unaccustomed to Forrest paying such close attention to my mood.

"Me neither, really," he said.

"Are you supposed to start a Blue Locker Society here, at Margaret Simon Middle School?"

"Yeah, I guess that's the idea. Get one going, so we have something to talk about at the conference."

I asked if he had other guys and if they had any idea how to set up a Web site. He said he was going to make Luke do it with him.

"You should ask Jake to be in it," I said.

"Why? Is he your boyfriend or something?"

"No. He's just a good guy and would do it, probably," I said.

"Everybody knows he likes you."

"Whatever. Moving on, what about setting up a Web site? Do you know how to do it?"

"We'll figure it out."

"And how will you let boys know that it exists? So they send in questions?"

Forrest shrugged. "They'll figure it out, I guess."

We talked some more and I told him about our PLS schedule and how we meet every school day. I talked about how we decide which questions to answer and what had been difficult so far.

"Mr. Ford said we can meet in the football coach's office during study hall. It's empty all afternoon," Forrest said.

I told him how a set place to meet was important and how we were finally back in our plush offices, after a stint in the basement.

"I remember going in that office with you," Forrest said.

"Yeah, that was forever ago," I said nonchalantly.

I wanted him to get that I was over him. Even though the getting over part was still in progress. I looked down at my bracelet. I tried to think of any neutral subject, anything other than my endless crush on him.

"Did I tell you my mom's having a baby?"

"Yes. You told me on New Year's Eve, remember?"

Great, from one uncomfortable subject to an even more uncomfortable subject—the night I stopped being his pretend girlfriend. I looked over at the clock above the gym door and pretended I had to get going, even though study hall was far from over.

"Okay, Forrest. Good luck with this. If you have other questions, you can ask Kate or Piper, too. They know just as much as me."

I had done it. I nearly pumped my fist in victory once I was outside the gym and out of sight. I spent time with Forrest and I didn't become a pile of mush. I didn't analyze his every word and I walked out first. I couldn't believe it: Was I finally over the biggest crush of my entire life?

Ten

When you add something new to a Web site, you can put it in big flashing letters so everyone immediately sees it. Or you can just put it off in its own little corner and see what happens. With the Period Predictor, we launched it big on www .pinklockersociety.org. We placed a grabby headline on the front page of the Web site, promising girls: "Get an answer—FINALLY—and FAST!"

Click on the button and girls could answer a short quiz and receive an estimate of when their first period would arrive. I was proud of how I based it on the real medical knowledge I now possessed. Developing from a girl into a woman happens in stages, I now knew. You don't go to bed flat-chested and wake up the next day with grown-up boobs. I had seen that in myself. It takes a while—like two years—for things to progress. And that was a key to our Period Predictor. Basically, you plug in the date you got your first bra and we add twenty-four to thirty months to that. *Voilà!* We have your answer.

I could hardly wait for the fan mail to start pouring in. Was there nothing the Internet couldn't do? What I didn't reveal was that I was the original test case. I put my information in and learned that I would be getting my period on March 21. Now that was just three days away! I could hardly wait. I carried my supplies with me every day to school. I was ready, ready to finally be growing up in that very clear and obvious way.

"Great news, Jemma," Kate said during the next Pink Locker Society meeting. "More than one hundred girls have already downloaded the Period Predictor. You are revolutionizing puberty!" she said.

"*We* are," I insisted, not wanting to take all the credit.

"Nice job," Piper said. "We should have charged them each a dollar."

"Piper!" Kate said.

"Just kidding," she said.

I agreed, though, and wondered if that's how businesses were born.

"Let's talk about the meeting," Kate said.

By that, she meant THE MEETING—our planned meeting with Ms. Russo and Mrs. Percy to spill the whole story to Principal Finklestein.

"I say we just get it over with, rip off the bandage," Piper said. "I'd do it today, if we could."

"What does Ms. Russo say?" I asked.

"She says she'll set it up for Thursday. We'll all go in. They'll start the conversation and we can just pipe in with comments," Kate said.

My stomach lurched as if we were at the top of the tallest roller-coaster hill ever. And did she really say Thursday, the very day the Period Predictor said I will get my first period? Bad timing, if you ask me. I had thought about whether I should just stay home from school that day. Now I'd have to go.

I could not see myself in that meeting "piping in" with anything. It was a comfort that my parents knew the truth, but I was still afraid of Principal Finklestein. In my mind, I tried to imagine a happy-ending version of our meeting. I saw us all in his office. First there was tension, then an explanation, then smiles and handshakes all around. Maybe Mrs. Percy and Ms. Russo would be so convincing it would all just take care of itself?

Eleven

As if we didn't have enough to talk about at the next Pink Locker Society meeting, we had a mountain of messages from girls, asking for help of all kinds. The usual was, of course, PBBs—periods, bras, and boys. But we had a new "B" entering the picture—bullies. One girl said a whole bunch of her former friends were giving her bullying stares all the time. They wouldn't talk to her and were giving her weird looks all the time. That would drive me crazy.

And another seventh-grade girl said some mean eighth-graders were pushing her out of her bus seat when they went around curves. We answered these questions and told them both to talk to the girls directly. If that didn't work, we said to talk to a parent or the school counselor. But then a message of a different sort came in. It was clear the writer was not going to ask an adult for help.

Dear PLS,

I don't like to ask for help, but here I am asking. I'm a pretty and popular person. You would never believe it if you knew who was writing this. But someone is making my life so hard. I want to stay home from school every day. I've even cried about it AT SCHOOL. I laugh it off and even tease the person back, but I can't do it anymore. It's just too hard. It was fine when she was making fun of my lip gloss or my boyfriend or whatever, but now she knows that I don't get good grades. I never have.

I've had tutors and special summer camps and everything, but it just doesn't work for me. I think probably I don't really need school because I'm sure I'll be a successful person at something glamorous. I have my looks. But I have to pass eighth grade. And right now, I'm not. I don't want to tell any teachers about this bully problem. Then a certain extremely tall and conceited person will tease me for being a snitch. And I can't tell my friends because I don't want them to know I'm flunking. What do I do?

Signed,
Student F

"What do we tell her?" Piper asked. "There's no answer. That mean girl is not going to stop."

"I wonder who it is?" I said, my mind ticking through the popular girls bold enough to assure us that she "has her looks." Then I ticked through a list of the tall girls at our school who could be the bully.

"Well, I don't know what to tell her," Kate said. "Let's at least say we support her."

"That doesn't seem like enough," I said.

"Well, it's all we have," Kate said.

"Let's tell her to ask her friends to help her," I said.

"But she doesn't want anyone to know," Piper said.

Was it enough just to be a cheerleader for this girl? I hoped so because that's all we offered Student F in our response. At least we answered her, I guess, before we moved on to making plans for the BIG MEETING. It was a day before Thursday.

Thursday, otherwise known as the day I was supposed to get my first period. We decided we each would have one point to discuss. I was supposed to talk about the number of girls we'd helped already— more than one hundred questions answered. Kate would stress the history of the PLS and the importance of continuing it. Piper would talk about the Internet's global reach and how our helpful advice

44

could spread far beyond the girls at Margaret Simon Middle School.

"*Magnifique!*" she said. "Our points are perfect."

During study hall, we filed nervously into Principal Finklestein's office. Ms. Russo and Mrs. Percy were already there.

Ms. Russo broke the ice and explained the purpose of the meeting, but the second she said "Pink Locker Society," the principal's expression went blank. Ms. Russo discussed the background of how the Pink Locker Society had originally begun, long ago, and how it could and should have a place in the future of Margaret Simon Middle School.

"I have to stop you right there, Jane. That club was banned months ago," he said.

"Yes, but what Jane's saying is that perhaps that decision could be reconsidered," Mrs. Percy said.

Principal Finklestein stopped and listened to Mrs. Percy's full sentence.

He let her continue. She laid out a logical case and a sound plan for allowing the Pink Locker Society to operate openly, just like any school club.

"The girls have really done an admirable job of answering questions, sending lifelines, if you will, to middle-school girls who are struggling," Mrs. Percy said. "Peer-to-peer counseling has merit, as you well know, according to all the latest education research."

More silence from Principal F., which we took as a good sign. I let my mind drift for a moment. A Pink Locker Society that didn't need to hide would be a glorious thing.

As he listened to Ms. Russo and Mrs. Percy, he would occasionally look at us. I smiled and nodded, feeling good about the direction we were heading. I looked at the note cards in my lap, ready to report on the hundred questions we'd already answered. I was going to speak after Piper. Feeling so upbeat now, I thought I might end my bit with "Girl power!"

Piper started in about the revolutionizing power of the Internet, but Principal Finklestein stopped her immediately and stood up.

"I'm sorry, Piper. I don't have any more time for this closed issue. My only decision now has to do with disciplinary matters," he said.

What?

Mrs. Percy gave it one more try, but he shut her down as well.

"Adele, you have my continued respect, as we've worked together for thirty years now, but I have the school district's reputation to consider. And my own.

"As I believe I've said before, we can't have children giving advice to other children about delicate issues."

Yes, he had said that, at my house, to my parents and everyone else's parents on that horrible day.

"They've been responsible in their duties," Ms. Russo said. "They've consulted the school nurse more than once."

"That's all well and good, but this Web site is nothing but one big risk," Principal F. said. "I don't have time to police every word on that Web site. Just like I don't have time to edit every single report from Bet Hirujadanpholdoi that runs on Margaret Simon TV."

"These girls can be trusted," Mrs. Percy said in a firm voice.

"Something goes haywire and you know who the TV news crews will be calling, don't you? I'm not losing my job over some half-baked attempt at 'girl power,'" he said, putting finger quotes around the words.

We all looked at the floor, feeling one hundred percent defeat. We looked up again when he said our names.

"Jemma, Piper, and Kate. Did I or did I not ask you to cease operating this Web site?"

"Y-yes, but . . . ," Kate began.

"Then you can understand why there is likely to be some punishment coming for disobeying me."

"What?" Ms. Russo said in disbelief.

"I can't rule it out," he said.

Twelve

Piper started asking questions of Ms. Russo even before we were fully ushered out of the principal's office. Mrs. Percy stayed behind for who-knew-what reason.

"Shhh!" Ms. Russo said, and shuffled us down the hall. Piper was livid.

"I cannot believe he wouldn't even listen to us. I swear he does not care at all about girls and he obviously doesn't respect 'the power of the global Internet,'" Piper said, using her own air quotes now.

Kate was surprised.

"I thought we'd at least have a chance to make our points," she said.

I was scared.

"What punishment does he mean? Detention? A suspension?"

Ms. Russo started talking, but honestly, I wasn't listening. My mind started to wander to whether he might just expel us from school entirely. Did this mean I would never go to college? OMG, maybe he was calling the police to get them involved. Could we be accused of fraud or something for taking that pink laptop back and not using it for homework, like he said?

And another thing: It was already after lunch and I still hadn't gotten my you-know-what. I would give it the whole day, of course, and I was mildly relieved it hadn't happened at school. It could have happened while sitting on the pale blue cushion of one of the chairs in the principal's office. But still, I wasn't happy. I thought this day would end with two major accomplishments. So far, it was holding at zero.

Kate must have sensed my silent panic and took me by both shoulders. She gave me a serious look. I guess you could say she snapped me out of it. I took a breath and started hearing what Ms. Russo was saying.

"This is just round one. We'll fight this," she said, but she had no energy in her voice.

"Fight it how?" Piper asked. "He said no and he's ready to bring the hammer down on us."

Kate said we should keep answering questions.

"He didn't tell us to stop," she said.

"Uh, he did tell us. Five months ago," I said.

Kate said she was not one for getting into trouble, but it didn't seem to her that we *could* get in much more trouble at this point.

Ms. Russo said we had to assume we were still presenting our Pink Locker Society session at Tomorrow's Leaders Today. She said she wished she had told "George" (aka Principal F.) about that.

"Maybe we should have told him about that. He loves when his school is recognized. But maybe he would have been even angrier," Ms. Russo said quietly, sounding like she was talking to herself. Then she snapped out of it and turned to us.

"By the way, how is Forrest doing with the Blue Locker Society? Does anyone know?"

When I told her we had talked, she said to keep helping him.

"Really, boys are clueless on this stuff," she said. "He needs all the help you can give him."

We looked up and saw Mrs. Percy heading toward us, a serious look on her face. Her sensible shoes pad-padded briskly down the hall. She gave us a reassuring look.

"Don't be alarmed but he's digging in his heels."

I reached out and touched her shoulder to get her attention.

"Are we getting suspended?"

"No," she said, but the look on her face stayed flat.

"Worse?" I asked.

She exhaled and told us that something important was now on the table.

"It's the class trip," she said. "He feels that would be an adequate punishment and wouldn't go on your permanent records."

The permanent record was something you could write off, but not when you were an eighth-grader who—weeks from now—would be applying to the best high school in the city. Mrs. Percy said she'd try to "work her magic" on the principal, but I couldn't put much faith in that. If he respected her so much, why had he come roaring at us with disciplinary action with her right there in the room?

I spent the rest of the afternoon in a fog. Whenever I saw Kate and Piper, we just kind of shook our heads at each other. We had been *tra-la-la*-ing down a certain path and now we had absolutely no idea where to go. I thought about telling my parents what happened, but instead I decided to do what everyone else was doing: hope that Principal Finklestein would change his mind.

Thirteen

I tensed up on Friday as soon as I heard the bell that signaled study hall. We had no assigned room for study hall to free us up for PLS business. But now that Principal F. knew what we were up to, we didn't know what to do. Should we roam the halls and get snagged for not having a pass? Or should we sneak through the pink locker doors and continue this rule-breaking activity? Personally, I thought about spending the entire period in the restroom awaiting my period. It had not come on Thursday as the Period Predictor said it would. I ran my information through it one more time and got the same result. Still. Waiting.

"Let's go, Jemma. No fear," Piper told me. She linked her arm in mine and marched me over to my locker.

"Meet ya in there," she said.

I twisted and turned the combination, checking over my shoulder twice before jumping in.

Kate was already there, curled up on the couch with the laptop.

"Come here, Jem," she said. Then, silently, she pointed to about ten new messages. They weren't new questions or the fan mail we were used to getting. They were complaints about the Period Predictor.

"This simply doesn't work," read one. "The Period Predictor is worse than a horoscope!" blared another. "I predict you will take this off your site," predicted another.

I threw my head back and looked at the ceiling as if it held an answer.

"This is your baby, Jem. Maybe you need to tweak it a bit, so it works better?" Kate said.

"I gave it my best shot," I said. "It should work, based on everything I know."

Kate nodded sympathetically.

"But it didn't even work for me," I admitted.

Kate raised her eyebrows.

"What's this now?" Piper asked.

"Nothing," I said.

"We're getting a few comments about the Period Predictor," Kate said.

"What do they say?" Piper said.

"They say it's not working, okay? I know, it's my fault."

"*Relaxez-vous*," Piper said. "I just wanted to know what you guys were talking about. I was worried it was more Principal F. nonsense."

"Well, this doesn't help," I said. "It's one thing to say we're providing this great service, but if people are complaining now . . ."

"Just a few are," Piper said. "Can't you fix it?"

"I guess I can try," I said.

"What's going on with the Blue Locker Society? Any more meetings with you-know-who?" Piper said with a sly glance.

"No. We just met one time."

"Don't you guys think we better take charge of the whole Blue Locker Society situation?" Kate said. "No offense, but Luke didn't know anything about it. Apparently, Forrest is the only member of the Blue Locker Society."

"Perfect, they have no members, no place to meet, no Web site, and no plan," Piper said.

"I guess I can talk to him," I said.

Both of them looked at me as if I was about to jump in the ocean without a life preserver.

"If you think I should, I mean," I said, trying to seem casual about it.

Fourteen

It would have been better if Forrest had started our conversation with a topic other than Taylor. But whatever. I kept my game face on as we met for meeting two in our usual spot on the gym bleachers. The sixth-graders were in full promenade.

"Is there a way to, you know, move her up your list, or whatever?"

I looked at him blankly. I couldn't fathom the thought that Taylor, in her perfect blondness, could ever need something from me.

"She was crying, you know, a few weeks ago."

That I remembered. Forrest comforting her at his locker.

He said, "She was crying at my locker again today. Clem's being a real, well, you know."

"Clem?"

"Yes, that's who's messing with her. She won't stop. I told her to write you guys."

"Taylor?"

"Yeah, she said she did. Wrote in about her problem."

Whoa. Taylor is Student F.

"I kind of promised that you'd help her. I said I could make it happen," Forrest said.

I told him how we sent our typical encouraging letter about being bullied. "We told her to tell an adult, have her friends stick by her, the usual," I said.

"Well, that's good. But she was still crying today."

"Maybe she's just trying to make you feel bad for her."

He rolled his eyes.

"I'm not into her anymore. You know that," he said.

I was tempted to ask who he was into these days, but instead I stared down at my soda tab bracelet and got back on track.

"I thought we were supposed to be talking about the Blue Locker Society. This conference is coming up and we have exactly nothing to say. No Power-Point. No nothing."

"I'm getting it together," Forrest said. "No sweat."

"Are you going to get any more members, or a place to meet?"

"Other guys, yeah. I do have a meeting place. Want to see it?"

And that's how I ended up on the roof of the school in the chilled March air with Forrest McCann. First, he led me to the second floor of our school, then to an alcove off the library, then to a closet in the alcove. Inside the closet was an iron ladder affixed to the wall, like we were in a submarine instead of a middle school.

"I thought you were supposed to use the football coach's office," I said.

"C'mon," he said.

Up the rungs we climbed, until we were at ceiling level and he pushed on a panel. It flipped open and let in a blast of daylight and the entire blue sky. He held his hand out as I took that first step, setting my first foot on the roof. I waved him off, but soon wished I had taken his hand. The surface was loose and pebbly so you never felt like you had your footing.

It turns out there's a tiny greenhouse up there, where our cooking teacher grows herbs. And a single chair, unexplained. Roofs are romantic places. I think it has something to do with the quiet up there. The view seems to want to whisper something to you. And nobody knows where you are. But I stuck to business.

We moved over to the greenhouse, where I could lean against a table and jot down notes. This was a fine enough place to meet, I told him, provided it wasn't snowing and the panel door didn't get frozen shut. Or locked? He had no information about the long-term access issues affecting the rooftop meeting place.

Forrest needed members now, I told him. And they needed to meet at least once a week, and most importantly, they needed to find a way to get questions from boys.

"If you can't do a Web site, then just have them write down questions in a notebook or something," I said.

"Guys aren't going to do that," he said.

"Well, how are you going to help boys if no one will say anything to anyone?"

"I think it's just the idea that a guy could ask something if he wanted to," Forrest said.

I shook my head and had to laugh. Would I ever understand boys? Oh sure, that would happen approximately never.

"Here's the thing, though, Forrest," I said. "What are we going to say at Tomorrow's Leaders Today?"

"I'll figure it out. We have time."

Then I told him about the whole Principal Finklestein fiasco and how the New York City trip itself was in possible jeopardy for me.

"You have to go. I can't go without you."

For a moment, I locked eyes with him, wondering what he meant.

"I mean, I can't give a whole talk about the Pink and Blue Locker Societies. What do I know about girls?"

Fifteen

*L*ife can surprise you, my mother is famous for saying. She's right, of course. But it's not always in a good way. A week to the day that we had our big meeting with the principal, he called us down to his office again. No Ms. Russo or Mrs. Percy this time.

We stood nervously like a trio of prisoners waiting for the bad news.

"I could suspend you but that would hurt your chances of getting into the best high school. And that's not fair to Margaret Simon, which has a reputation for turning out scholars."

"Thank you. Jemma and I are applying to Charter," Kate said, her eyes brightening.

"I am, however, forbidding you from attending the school field trip."

Stomachs lurched. Tears sprang to our eyes. But Principal F. hustled us out of his office before we could collect ourselves and make further arguments. We were whisked back into the hallway and pointed toward the eighth-grade hall.

Stunned, we walked back to class, slow as elephants.

"What about the Tomorrow's Leaders Today conference?" Piper said.

"I think we can forget about that," I said.

"This so stinks," Piper said. "I have been doing research about French restaurants, French boutiques, and even a French movie theater we can go to in New York."

"We'll have to find something fun to do together while everyone else is in New York. A sleepover?" Kate said.

No one had the heart to say how lame that sounded in comparison to staying with your friends in a big city.

After school, I couldn't bring myself to tell my parents. I knew I would have to eventually. But right now, it hurt too much. I tried to keep to myself, but my mother had news of her own. She pulled me out of my room and into the kitchen.

"Have a snack," she said, pointing me toward some fruit salad on the counter. Glumly, I plucked out a green slice of kiwi and nibbled at it.

"Jemma," she said, "I went to the doctor today . . ."

"Is everything okay?" I asked, gulping the rest of the kiwi.

"Oh my, yes. I'm doubly sure of that." She wore a big smile and seemed a little out of breath.

"What then, did you finally find out if it's a boy or a girl?"

"No, we're still holding firm on that."

"What then?"

"It turns out we're going to have . . . twins!"

She waited for my reaction, which was delayed, maybe because of the rough day I had. But I couldn't not react to this. This was huge and I was happy in a holy-moley-what-will-happen-next-in-my-life sort of way.

Within moments, I posted the news on my Facebook page and the comments came flying in. I got some LOLs when I explained that the doctors called it a "hidden twin." You wouldn't think that there'd be room in the uterus to hide, but there you go. My friends were pretty quick to start suggesting names. Eddie and Betty, Jilly and Milly, Jack and Jill, and my personal favorite, Stop and Go. Bet chimed in with Jaidee for a girl and Jai for a boy. She also added: *Call me.* Which I did.

Kate had told her about our confrontation with Principal F. and she wanted to know more.

"This kind of involves me, too," Bet said. "Because I have a never-before-seen *You Bet!* broadcast about the Pink Locker Society."

We had posted her video on the PLS Web site, but it wasn't the same as showing it to the whole school over MSTV. I heavily doubted Principal F. was about to change his mind about letting her show that report.

"I think you can forget about that, Bet," I told her as we sat outside Lucky's Coffee Shop. The April sun was strong and it warmed you in an almost-summery way. I lifted my sunglasses from my face and positioned them as a headband. I told her, in a quiet voice, about how we'd been banned from the New York City trip.

"That is such complete nonsense," Bet said. "We have to do something."

"But what?" I said.

"Sometimes you just have to make a fuss. Then you figure it out."

We drained our cups of Earl Grey tea and talked

about the babies. Everyone wanted to talk about the babies.

My parents were adjusting to the news and buying two of everything. I was still happy to become a big sister. But if I was wary of one new baby in the house, imagine how I felt knowing that there would be two of them. I wanted to be helpful to my parents, but I sort of wondered whether my social life was about to take a serious nosedive. I would obviously be needed as a babysitter. Were my weekends about to be awash in diapers and bottles?

More and more of me didn't mind, though. When I'd see a cute baby at the library or the store, I would just light up inside. I tried to smile at every baby I met, testing my charm on the toothless and adorably bald. I had a pretty good record. Much better than I did with cute boys. But then again, I didn't make funny faces at the boys or tickle their toes.

We left Lucky's and went across to the park that has a gazebo in the middle. We sat inside because it's a great spot to talk. It's also a great spot for people watching. Boys played football in view of the gazebo and everybody included the park on their bike rides through the neighborhood.

"I just cannot wait until the babies are born," Bet said. "I will help you babysit anytime."

Just as I was about to accept, a football landed inside the gazebo and bounced off the table we were sitting at. Luke Zubin appeared, grabbed the football, then plunked himself down at our table.

"Jake's here, too," Luke said, gesturing over his shoulder. I looked over and saw Jake standing there. When he saw me, he gave me an awkward wave.

"What are we talking about, ladies?" Luke said.

Never shy, he spread his elbows out, exactly like my mother said you're not supposed to. We laughed because we were surprised to see him and also because he called us "ladies." That was grandpa speak.

"We were just talking about Jemma's twins."

"Jemma's having twins?"

"Luuuuuuke," I said.

"Oh yeah, I know. It's your mom. Did you tell her how I suggested Stop and Go?"

"I did, but she's not accepting traffic signals as baby names," I said.

"Did you hear about Taylor?" Luke asked.

"What is it?" Bet said.

"She's moving schools," Luke said. "She said she's going to West Fallows High School next year."

"Why would she go there?" Bet said. "It's ten miles from here. And it's not her district."

"Dunno," Luke said. "She probably has a boyfriend there or something."

"Taylor has a boyfriend?" I asked hopefully.

"Probably," he said. "Great seeing you ladies."

Again with the "ladies." Bet turned to me and said, "Taylor Mayweather. Didn't she used to go out with . . ."

"Yes, she did. And no, I don't like him anymore."

Sixteen

The next time my mom had a doctor appointment, I offered to go. These were pretty basic visits usually, and I liked knowing how big the babies were getting. My mom was getting pretty big, too, but she continued to eat a healthy diet. I never caught her with her spoon in the ice cream in the middle of the night, but I did catch her eating more than one grapefruit at a time.

The doctor saved the best part of the appointment for last. He held his stethoscope to Mom's belly and the fast *whoosh-whoosh* of their heartbeats filled the exam room. Hearing their hearts made the whole thing seem more real: My mom was really having twins—and soon. Her due date was in June, a little over two months away.

I had a sneaky reason for wanting to come along on this particular visit, though. Weeks had passed since my period was supposed to come, according to the Period Predictor. We had taken the P. Predictor off the Pink Locker Society site—temporarily, I hoped. That stopped the complaints, but it didn't stop me from wondering why my plan had failed. Did everything about growing up have to be so confusing and hard to pin down?

What I hadn't counted on today, though, was that my mother's doctor would be a dude. There were a lot of female doctors at this particular office, but when you were having a baby, you saw whichever one was free for regular appointments. I wanted to get a doctor's advice, a doctor who was an expert in female parts and processes. I was very close to letting Dr. Adams walk out of the room, but I got a burst of courage and leaped up from my plastic chair.

"Um, Dr. Adams? Can I ask you a question—a puberty question?"

My mother looked surprised, but she didn't interrupt.

"My pediatrician told me that a girl gets her period about two years after she starts, you know, getting developed in the chest area. I'm confused because it's been more than two years for me and still no period."

Dr. Adams stopped for a minute and said that sounded exactly right.

"So what's the deal, then?" I asked.

"I think the variable that's hard to pin down here is when exactly chest development occurs," he said.

"Well, I've been wearing a bra for exactly two and a half years," I said.

"There you go, then. When a girl wears a bra and when a girl *needs* to wear a bra because chest development has progressed to a certain point—those are two different things," he said.

I stood there almost stunned by my mistake.

"Thank. You," I said.

I had built the Period Predictor around that very question—when did the girl start wearing a bra? But that's just whenever, really. I started wearing a bra because all of my friends were and I didn't want to be the only one not wearing one. Now, when did I need to start wearing a bra? That I never really put on the calendar.

"Is everything all right, Jem?" Mom asked as we packed up and left the doctor's office.

Yes, I nodded. Fine. Based on what the doctor had

said, I wasn't sure at all that I'd be able to fix the Period Predictor. It was good to know where I went wrong, but it's another thing altogether to know how to fix it.

Seventeen

Dear PLS,

OK, so thanks for answering my letter. But I can't thank you for helping me. The conceited, mean girl who's bothering me won't stop. I sometimes don't even want to get up in the morning, knowing I'll see her and she'll say something. And I can't/won't do the stuff you suggest—telling an adult and asking my friends to stick with me. I'm independent and I don't want to be a crybaby.

I can't tell my friends because I don't want them to know I'm flunking almost every class. I'm desperately afraid you-know-who will tell the whole school. I sooooooooooo wish she hadn't found out in the first place.

Our very good taste in backpacks is to blame. Both our bags are made of Italian leather—mine is cerulean blue and hers is sort of a sky blue and we got them mixed up. I took hers and found it filled with high-priced cosmetics and a flat iron. She took mine and apparently rifled through everything, including all the failing test papers crumpled in the bottom.

She's still mad at me for something that happened months ago. OMG, how she loves knowing this secret about me. Sometimes it's less about what she says and more about how she looks at me. Like when a teacher says, "Does anyone have any questions?" she looks right at me, like she's saying "Don't you have any questions?"

Until now, I'd hidden it perfectly. When test papers were returned, I usually just folded them in half really fast and plunged them into my backpack. There are more in there now than ever before because I have kind of stopped trying. Once the school told my parents that I'd have to repeat eighth grade, what was the point? I don't even know if I'll be allowed to go on the eighth-grade trip. It's supposed to be a celebration, right? And what do I have to celebrate?

I started telling people I'm going to a high school outside of our school district. It will buy me some time. Then I figure I can tell them I transferred back in. What I really hope is that somehow I can repeat eighth

grade and be miraculously placed in tenth grade the next
year. Or maybe there's some summer school solution no
one's thought of. It could happen. Well, I'm hoping it can.

Signed,
Student F

It was a sign of how bad Taylor's situation was that even I felt sorry for her. If you had told me six months ago that I'd be trying hard to think of ways to help Taylor Mayweather, I would have told you that you were crazy.

"Just goes to show," Kate said. "No matter how well you have people figured out, you never know what's going on in their real lives."

"What a witch," Piper said.

"Which one?" I said sarcastically.

"The bully, of course, Jem," Kate said.

"I don't exactly love Taylor," Piper said. "Not after what she did to the PLS. But you've got to feel bad for her."

"Imagine what it would feel like to be flunking eighth grade," Kate said. "But I was always a little angry that she didn't get punished for hacking into the PLS site."

"I was really angry and still am, if I let myself think about it long enough," I said.

"*Exactement!*" Piper said.

"If that means 'exactly' in French, I agree. Who else completely tears people apart and gets away with it?" I said.

Taylor had admitted hacking into our site and making rude comments. She said people who wrote in to us were losers—so mean!

"And now here she is asking us for help," I said.

"Kind of ironic, don't you think?" Kate asked. "Taylor's famous for messing with other people and now someone is messing with her."

"Is it karma, do you think?" Piper asked. "What goes around, comes around?"

Eighteen

Sometimes the answer is so obvious, you just whack yourself in the forehead with the back of your hand and say, OK—I get it! I give in. Fine. Whatever.

That's how I felt about Jake Austin. Jake had liked me for months—maybe longer. I was more and more sure he was the person who sent me that note-less pink carnation on Valentine's Day. And he always seemed to find ways to say hi or try and make me laugh. I felt a little like my mother when she tears around the house looking for her reading glasses only to find they are sitting on top of her silly head. Here I was wondering what it was like to have a real boyfriend, someone who truly liked me.

I realized I could just say OK and be Jake's girl-friend.

My Forrest thoughts were truly fading, so I wasn't using Jake to get over him. I had gotten myself over Forrest and had been faithful to the goals I set for myself with the soda tab bracelet that was still on my wrist.

I had kept the promise I made to myself about not thinking about Forrest like I used to. It worked. I did other stuff. I had room for other thoughts. And with all the clutter cleared away, one of those thoughts was now about Jake Austin. Other girls liked him. He wasn't Mr. Most Popular, but he was Mr. Actually Pays Attention to Me. I didn't stay up nights writing about him in my journal. And I didn't stress about what I looked like when I bumped into him. He was my science lab partner and it was no big deal. He was smart and easy to be around.

So sort of like a science experiment, I started being nice back. I started acting a little more like Piper than myself. "Oh-ho, Jake," I said, laying a hand on his shoulder. "You are too funny."

He suddenly stood up straighter. He was shocked. He blushed. Later, he texted me. Out of the blue with some concocted story that he needed something for our science homework about frog anatomy. I didn't buy it. And when I texted back, I used a winky emoticon.

That weekend, he liked every status update and photo I added to Facebook. It was almost too easy. I was making myself pretty sick, but I decided to keep on with it. If I could spend years liking Forrest, surely I could convince myself to like someone who actually liked me.

The next day, Jake came up to our lunch table, his empty tray in hand.

"Hey," he said to the entire group.

He received heys in return and then he said, "Jemma, do you want to go outside?"

"*Oh-la-la*," Piper said.

"Um, sure," I said, and stood up and pushed in my chair.

My heart was beating, but not like it did when I used to go on dates with Forrest. They weren't real dates, of course, because I was his pretend girlfriend. But still, we sat together at movies, held hands, and kissed in Clem Caritas's backyard. My heart pounded because I didn't know what I had gotten myself into. Outside, we sat on the wall by the basketball court. I kept my hands in my jeans pockets, even though it was late April, sunny and warm.

"You should come to the baseball game after school. Lots of people go," Jake said.

"Um, sure. That would be fun. I could stop by after cross-country."

I wondered what I was supposed to do. Cheer for him? Smile and wave? I hadn't ever been anyone's real girlfriend before.

"Can I ask you something, Jake?"

He nodded and I had to ask.

"Did you send me a carnation on Valentine's Day?"

"Do you think I did?" Jake said, giving me a smile.

"Yeah, I think you did."

"Well, maybe I did," he said.

And that, in my mind, was the end of that.

I went to the baseball game, dragging Kate along with me, even though that meant she had to wait around after dance practice for me to be done running. We walked down the big hill together. The sun was getting low on the horizon, but it was still warm, hinting at the summer to come. The team's uniforms blazed white against the green grass and the red dirt of the base paths. Someone was playing "before the game" music over the scratchy PA system. A wafty popcorn and hot dog smell floated through the air.

We took seats on the bleachers amid parents and other fans there to watch the boys. When Jake got up to bat, we did cheer: "C'mon, Austin!" and "Let's go, Patriots!" since we were the Margaret Simon Middle School Patriots.

I cheered for everyone equally so it wouldn't seem too obvious. When Forrest came up to bat, I didn't know what to do. But, to be consistent, I cheered for him, too. Kate joined in, being an equal opportunity cheerer anyway. "Let's go Forrest!" I yelled. And it was at that moment that Jake looked over from second base, which he had stolen. I wondered what Jake knew or assumed about me and Forrest. I could tell Jake how I didn't think of Forrest at all anymore. Well, hardly at all. But it seemed better just to ignore the whole matter.

I didn't plan to ask Jake about Francine DeBusey, the cute seventh-grader he had been going out with before Christmas. I wasn't even a tiny smidge jealous. It didn't seem like a great sign, but maybe Jake and I could be a couple in a new, super-mature way. I couldn't imagine Jake ever making me cry. Maybe we could just pass on the drama. We'd have no silly fights about who was supposed to text whom. We'd also skip the jealous moments just because he talked to a girl who happened to be a friend or vice versa for mc with a guy friend. I had never seen it done before, but there was always a first time.

Nineteen

emma Colwin, please report to the office.
"Piper Pinsky, please report to the office.
"Kate Parker, please report to the office."

Our heads popped up one by one from the Spanish quiz we were taking.

We looked around, nervous as kindergartners not knowing what to do next.

"Finish your quizzes," Señora Parra said.

I sped through the verb conjugations, forgetting more than I knew before I heard that distressing call over the PA system. We handed in our quizzes and gathered our stuff.

"This can't be good," I said.

"We already lost the class trip," Piper said. "What else could happen?"

"Maybe it's not so bad," Kate said.

"I think we're going to get in trouble because the PLS site is still up and running," I said.

We walked briskly to the office, expecting to be hustled into Principal Finklestein's office. Instead, Mrs. Percy greeted us from across the big front desk.

"Hello, girls. Let's go in the conference room."

Ms. Russo was already there. As we took our seats, Mrs. Percy told us that the principal was away at a conference.

"So it seemed like a good time to check in and check up," she said.

"I was hoping you were going to say we could go on the class trip. Maybe Principal F. changed his mind?" Piper said.

"I wish we had that kind of news," Ms. Russo said.

"What kind of news do you have?" Kate asked.

"We wanted to encourage you to keep the PLS Web site running, as you have been," Mrs. Percy said. "Though things look dark now, we still have hope that the PLS can continue next year at Margaret Simon Middle School."

"Yes, we need to appoint seventh-graders who can take over for you next year," Ms. Russo said. "So let us know if you have any nominations."

That was weird to think about. I wasn't ready to let go of the PLS yet, and I was nervous. I wanted to keep it running for the rest of the school year. (We didn't want to let all those girls down.) But we had to seriously cross our fingers that Principal F. would never actually go to www.pinklockersociety.org and see we had completely ignored his orders. Again.

"But we also wanted you to know that it's especially important for you to lay low right now," Ms. Russo said.

"Meaning what?" I asked.

"You don't want to risk getting suspended," Mrs. Percy said. "And I fear that's what Principal Finklestein would do if he caught you red-handed, or should I say pink-handed?"

"*Très amusante*," Piper said.

I was not so amused.

"Do you think he suspects anything?" I asked Mrs. Percy.

"I don't know. All he would tell me was the official reason he listed for banning you from the class trip."

"Because we restarted the PLS when he told us not to, right?" I asked.

"Not exactly. The official school rule you broke was operating a student club without being officially sanctioned."

"Sanctioned?" Kate asked.

"Sanctioned is another way of saying 'approved.' All school clubs are officially approved at one point or another," Mrs. Percy said. "Many have been sanctioned for decades, like *le club Francais*, a club Piper is probably well acquainted with."

"*Oui*," said Piper. French for *yes* pronounced "we."

A sanctioned club has a charter (a document that explains the rules), a designated teacher-advisor, and signed permission forms from parents to let their kids be in it, Mrs. Percy explained. "I guess the PLS has always been a secret group without official approval."

"Can we get sanctioned? Ms. Russo has been our teacher-advisor. And we could write a charter," Kate asked.

"I'm afraid it would be difficult now. Principal Finklestein and the school board would have to recommend it for sanctioning. It's hard to get a new club sanctioned or an old club unsanctioned," Mrs. Percy said. "Lots of paperwork."

"Couldn't we at least try?" Piper said.

Ms. Russo and Mrs. Percy exchanged glances but neither said anything. Which in a way did answer Piper's question, and that answer was "No."

Twenty

After school, I nearly dove into my running clothes and sprinted out to the track to start my run. I didn't want to talk to my teammates or my coach or take the long way around to catch a glimpse of the baseball team.

"Want to run together?" Mimi Caritas asked me. Clem's younger sister looked up to me, I knew. She joined the track team when I told her, "If I can distance run, you can distance run." She was doing great, actually. But today, I just didn't want the company.

"I'm sorry, Mimi. I'm upset about something and I wouldn't be a good partner."

I felt like if I could run, I could erase the noise and

worries filling my head. At mile one, the anxiety had lifted only slightly. All thoughts kept leading me back to our troubling situation—no class trip and a grim future for the PLS.

Though I kept hoping for some miracle to occur, it was now clear that nothing would change. I'd have to tell my parents that I wouldn't be going to New York. Class trips can't be replaced, I thought. There are very few of them and hardly any are overnight, stay-at-hotel trips. When else are you going to get to go somewhere fun with your close friends and the entire eighth grade? And when else would I get to visit New York City, the city that never sleeps? Fashion, art, theater, hot dogs on every street corner—it was all there for the taking.

Missing the class trip meant missing our chance to make a presentation at the Tomorrow's Leaders Today conference, too. Someone would have to tell Forrest. Would he go on without me? It was hard to imagine him making the presentation alone. I wondered how many Blue Locker Society meetings had been held on the roof since he took me up there.

Then there was the larger problem of the Pink Locker Society's future. Should we keep putting ourselves at risk by running the Web site until we graduated eighth grade? At first, I couldn't imagine giving up on our work or passing along our positions and our offices to unknown seventh-grade girls. But the idea was growing on me.

I think that's when I started to understand what the word *bittersweet* meant. It was sad (bitter) to think about leaving the PLS behind, but somehow happy (sweet) to think about this great tradition continuing. To quote Mrs. Percy, it was a chance to actually be "a link in a pink chain."

But right now, everything seemed uncertain.

Working through all these thoughts, I lost track of how many times I had run our circuit. I'd gone up hills and by the baseball fields I don't know how many times. My legs were aching and I suddenly wanted to stop running. The sky had darkened when I made it to the doors of the gym. Mimi was already dressed and walking out to the parking lot.

"Jemma, how far did you go today? No one could catch you and it was like you didn't even notice."

"Sorry, I'm in my own world today."

"Well, if you need someone to talk to, you can ask me. I'm a good listener," Mimi said. "Just yesterday, my sister was telling me about this boy, Shane, who she really likes, but who is majorly into Tayor Mayweather."

"I know you're a good listener, Mimi," I said. "We'll run together tomorrow."

Twenty-one

A s I watched my large-bellied mom make breakfast, I thought about how I didn't know much
about pregnancy before. Now, with the due date edg-
ing closer, I knew plenty. I knew my mom was having
trouble sleeping at this late stage. I knew that she had
heartburn when she ate pizza. I learned that women
don't get a period while they're pregnant (who knew?).
And I found out that you didn't want the babies to be
born too early because their lungs were still developing. It was seven weeks and counting for the Colwin
Twins.

My mind drifted again, like it had all of yesterday,
to my own twin worries: the PLS's future and having
to tell my parents about the lost school trip. If you

threw in Jake, you could have called them my triplet dilemmas. Toss in my period, which still hadn't come, and we'd have quadruplet troubles.

I thought for a moment about saying something to Mom about what was on my mind, but I just couldn't do it. She looked happy, humming something as she scrambled my cooking eggs in the nonstick pan. She was probably thinking about what else she needed to buy before the babies were born. It was an activity that was taking up most of our weekends.

"I heard about the New York City problem, by the way," she said, still stirring the eggs.

"What?"

"Ms. Russo called. She just feels terrible. And I feel terrible that you girls are going to miss out."

"It's completely unfair," I said, relieved she didn't seem too angry.

"Well, it's better than a suspension, I guess. You're learning the tough lesson of what it means to go out on a limb for something."

"The limb crashed to the ground, with me on it," I said. "We don't know what to do, actually."

"Ms. Russo said not to lose hope. She and Mrs. P. are still working on the principal. He might change his mind."

"Sure," I said, not really believing it.

"I could come in and talk to him," she said.

"Please don't."

"Well, I would have, but Ms. Russo said it probably wouldn't do any good."

"Right," I said.

"You know, your father and I could always take you to New York at some future point."

I pictured the three of us in Times Square with two adorable but screaming babies.

"Right," I said again.

I finished my eggs and orange juice and headed for the bus stop. When I arrived at school, Bet was waiting for me at my locker.

"What's the latest?" she said.

"Nothing good, I'm afraid," I said.

"So I heard," Bet said. "I'm planning on interviewing Principal F., you know."

"Ask him why I can't go to New York City. On second thought, don't."

"I have to interview him because he's celebrating forty years of working at Margaret Simon Middle School," Bet said.

"Oh, joy."

"Yes, it's a dull reason, I know," Bet said. "But I'm going to ambush him with some other topics. I have been digging around in the school records and I may have something that will help the PLS."

"What kind of something?"

"I don't want to say until I get more info—and talk to the big guy."

"Good luck with that," I said.

"Hey, Jemma." It was Forrest, pulling open his locker next to mine, like he did every morning.

I smiled at him and turned back to continue my talk with Bet. Then I heard another voice over my shoulder.

"Jemma, hey." It was Jake.

He hugged me hello, which was kind of a normal thing at my school. It didn't exactly mark us as boy-friend and girlfriend, but it was an awfully warm greeting for an ordinary Wednesday.

"Oh, hey. Hi, Jake," I said, returning the hug, but only briefly. I thought I could feel Forrest looking at us, but it could have been my imagination.

"Coming to my game on Friday?" Jake asked.

"Yeah, sure. I guess," I said.

"Cool," he said, and walked off to class.

"I'm pitching," Forrest said, more to his locker than to me.

"What?" I said.

Bet, seeing me caught up in yet another conversa-tion, smiled, waved, and headed off to class herself.

"I'm pitching," Forrest said. "I didn't pitch the last game you were at."

"Well, good luck, then. For Friday."

"Thanks," he said, and smiled.

Twenty-two

Weary of always running from the law—or at least the law handed down by Principal F.—we decided to meet officially only once a week. So our deluxe office sat empty every day except Wednesday. It wasn't that we didn't have a ton of Pink Locker work piling up. But the fewer chances to get caught climbing in and out of our lockers, the better. We were trying to keep the Pink Locker Society running while staying as invisible as possible.

We also decided to permanently set the date on the Web site's main page to March 21, when we had had our meeting with Principal F. Then, if he ever checked, it would always look like we hadn't touched the Web site since he confronted us about it.

But in truth, we continued to answer questions. We had been handling the usual questions about bra cup sizes, leg shaving, and all matters boy-related. Periods remained a popular topic and I relaunched the Period Predictor after making some "improvements." I was living proof that we really couldn't narrow it down to the exact day that a girl would get her first period. Instead, we gave an estimated six-month range—and even that we had to say was just a rough estimate. It was not the crystal-clear answer girls were looking for, but it was medically correct, the school nurse and my mother's doctor had assured me.

We also started getting a rash of new questions about the NYC trip. This made us deeply depressed, but we answered them. A lot of it had to do with friends squabbling about who was going to share a hotel room with whom. Two girls wrote in saying they were scared to be out of town without their parents. Discussing the subject left all three of us upset all over again. We used our conference call phone to dial Mrs. Percy's extension.

"We're sorry to bother you, Mrs. P., but can you talk to us?" Piper said.

Piper covered the receiver and said Mrs. Percy would be on as soon as she moved to a private spot to talk. Piper pressed the speakerphone button so we all could hear.

"Yes, girls. How can I help you today?"

"We are all just so . . . so upset about the trip. Is there anything at all that you can do?" Piper said.

"Ms. Russo and I are just torn up about it as well. In fact, she contacted Tomorrow's Leaders Today intending to say you girls couldn't be there and they told her that the Pink Locker Society is up for a major student leadership award."

"What?" I said.

"Yes, evidently it's a big deal. They nominate student groups appearing at the conference and one of them gets to represent Tomorrow's Leaders Today at their international conference," Mrs. Percy said.

"OMG," said Piper.

"Yes, that was Ms. Russo's reaction, too. So she just couldn't bring herself to pull you guys out of the lineup just yet."

"Couldn't we just go to New York on our own?" Kate said.

"Yes, we thought about that, but if Principal F. found out, Jane—I mean Ms. Russo—and I could lose our jobs."

"The New York trip is next week. Time is running out for us," I said.

"Let's not lose hope and let's look ahead. Have you identified any candidates yet?"

I nominated Mimi Caritas and Piper recommended Shannon Andersen, the student council rep who had passed out the carnations on Valentine's Day. Kate and Piper seconded the nominations.

"Excellent, Jemma. Time marches on and the Pink Locker Society will, too."

Then Mrs. Percy hung up the phone and we were alone again.

"I hope she's right," Piper said. "If I don't go on that New York trip, I think I'm going to lose it."

"I know," I said. "I want to scream when I hear people talking about the clothes they're packing or whether they're brave enough to go to the top of the Empire State Building."

"Maybe we should plan an alternate activity," Kate said, "just in case, so we're not too upset if the trip really does happen without us."

"No thanks," Piper said. "It'd be no fun if we're sitting around playing Scrabble when everyone we know is having the time of their lives."

The bell was ringing to signal the end of study hall. With the call to Mrs. Percy, we lost track of time. Quickly, we gathered our stuff and stepped inside our lockers. While standing there, I started to wonder if it was the end-of-study-hall bell I heard or the start-of-the-next-class bell. I hadn't checked a clock or my phone.

I almost flung open my locker door but I remembered how important it was not to get caught, with all that was at risk right now. I stood quietly, listening to the sounds outside in the locker block. First it was general murmuring as people gathered books and chatted, moving to their next class. Then it grew quiet, but I couldn't jump out because I still heard a voice. Then two voices. Then those voices were clearly arguing. At least one of them was.

"Pass any tests lately?" the voice said. "Shane thought you were smart, but I told him the truth."

"Whatever, Clem."

It was Clem, in the act: She was bullying Taylor.

"Seriously, I think he just likes dumb girls. That's what somebody told me," Clem said.

"Let me go to class," Taylor said.

"Why even bother? Aren't you flunking everything?"

There was no answer from Taylor and my heart went out to her. I pictured her frozen outside my locker. Cute, blond, and occasionally mean herself, even Taylor didn't deserve this.

"Can't think of anything to say back?" Clem said.

I flung open my locker, stepped out, and gave Clem my best glare.

"Oh, my God, Jemma. What are you doing?"

"Bully police."

"What?" Taylor said.

"I'm supposed to report bullying to the principal because it's such a big deal now."

"So you hide in lockers?" Clem asked. "You know, this isn't the first time I've seen you hide in a locker."

It was true, and Taylor had broadcast videotaped proof of me doing it. This reminded me of why I didn't like Taylor. But I tried to remind myself that I didn't have to love Taylor to help her escape a bullying situation.

"Whatever, Clem," I said.

"This is too weird," Clem said. "I'm going to class."

We watched her walk down the hall, her stick-straight blond hair swishing across her back as she went.

"Aren't you going to be late?" Taylor asked. She looked both embarrassed and relieved.

"It's okay. I have an extra hall pass," I said.

In fact, I had a stack of them for PLS-related work. This qualified.

"I don't understand why you were in your locker. Or why you helped me," Taylor said.

"Think pink," I said, then quickly turned down the hallway toward my class.

I know I left her shaking her head, but I knew she

would figure it out. I felt a little like a superhero who has left a calling card. I was like Batman flashing that bat flashlight of his into the night sky.

Sure, Taylor might tell everyone I was in the Pink Locker Society. But with so little time left in the year, and so much uncertainty, it felt like a risk worth taking.

Twenty-three

Watching Jake (and Forrest) play baseball that Friday gave me a lengthy opportunity to think through all my boy issues. Nine innings' worth.

"Kate, seriously, let's compare and contrast."

"Not this again," Kate said.

We had become pros at attending middle-school baseball games. We now brought a blanket so we could spread out under the sun, like it was the beach. We also could position ourselves far enough away from everyone else to have a talk like this.

"Jake is a little shorter, but some might say his face is cuter," I said.

"Forrest is taller and he's more of a scruffy guy," Kate said. "Jake pays attention to his hair and his clothes. Remember when he wore that pink polo shirt?"

"Yeah. You wouldn't catch Forrest in pink."

"How about brains? Which one gets better grades?" Kate asked.

"I'm guessing they're about even, but Forrest forgets stuff more. You know, he's kind of spacey," I said.

"Yeah, he once forgot that you were his girlfriend," Kate said, elbowing me.

"You're funny. We weren't really going out, so that doesn't count."

"You've come a long way, Jem. But even though I know you are not obsessing over Forrest anymore, I think this is a bad road—comparing him to Jake. And when it's during a game, it's like you're comparing stats from the backs of their baseball cards."

"It's hard to compare them actually, since Forrest is a pitcher and Jake is more of an outfielder."

"Thank you, sportscaster Jemma. You know what I mean."

I guess I did. I kept hoping that if I studied the situation long enough I'd figure it out. And what I was trying to figure out was why, after several weeks of basically being Jake's girlfriend, I still didn't think I liked Jake. Not in that way, anyway. He hadn't kissed me and I was afraid that he would. I wasn't that afraid about kissing. I figured I could kiss someone without making a fool of myself. But I was afraid that it wouldn't be nearly as nice as kissing Forrest.

But I did like Jake, as a person. So why was liking Jake so different from liking Forrest? What I really wanted to know is when I would meet someone who was not Forrest that I would have Forrest-like feelings for.

I told Kate I'd close the subject for the next forty-eight hours and give her a break.

"Thank you very much," she said. "It will give me a chance to tell you about my latest Zumba class." Kate had gone head over heels for dance. She was on the dance troupe at school and, whenever she could make it, she took dance classes at the Y. She stood up on our blanket and started demonstrating a tango-type move. She took a long blade of grass and held it like a rose in her teeth.

"I just wish I had music," Kate said. "You try it."

No way was I trying that move, barefooted, on our baseball beach blanket, in front of the rest of the baseball spectators. I was grateful I had decided to stay seated because Taylor Mayweather appeared on the edge of our blanket.

"Hi, Taylor," Kate said. "Want to sit with us?"

"I actually wanted to talk to Jemma a minute."

"Okay, sure," I said.

We walked a few paces away toward a weeping willow tree.

"I don't know how you knew to be in your locker at that very moment, but thank you."

"I was in my locker by total accident."

"Why is it that you sometimes go into your locker and close the door? It is unusual, you know?"

"I know. I know. I don't just stand in my locker with the door closed. I was coming back from somewhere."

"You said 'Think pink'! Does it have something to do with the Pink Locker Society? That's what they always say. I love that Web site."

"Maybe," I said.

"No way!" Taylor said, grabbing me by the shoulders, an OMG look on her face.

"Shhh!" I said.

Taylor lowered her voice and leaned in closer to say, "I still don't know where you could have been going to or coming from in your locker."

"I can't really say."

"Well then, can I ask how you got to be in the Pink Locker Society? I don't remember, like, an open audition or anything," Taylor said.

"It wasn't like that."

"Lucky you and whoever else is in it. My mother keeps saying I'd do better in school if I was involved in something. But I'm bad at sports."

"I used to think I was bad at sports, but now I'm running. You should try it."

"Maybe."

"Have things with Clem been any better?"

"It's only been two days, but maybe. I think you scared her, you know? I'm worried about the class trip, though," Taylor said.

"You're still going, right?"

"I don't know. She might just hassle me the whole time. It will be easier for her to corner me when we're out of town and the teachers are all distracted," Taylor said.

The idea of anyone voluntarily not going on the New York trip amazed me.

"You have to go. Don't miss it. Not for that reason, anyway."

Taylor just shrugged.

"Clem's smart. Another week will pass and she'll figure out that you're not really the bully police," she said.

"Well, I still think you should go. How many chances do you have to go on our eighth-grade field trip?"

As soon as I said it, I wanted to reel my words back in like a big dumb fish.

"Ha-ha. Well, this won't be my only chance, I guess," Taylor said.

"Oh, jeez. I am so sorry. I can't believe I said that."

"It's okay, really. I have to get used to it, I guess," Taylor said.

I thought about telling her how I wasn't going to be going even once, but I decided to keep it to myself.

Twenty-four

As the field trip drew closer, Kate, Piper, and I plunged deeper into sadness. I had accepted it on one level. But it was hard to take the buzz of energy I felt at school from all those eighth-graders who were going. Some of them had been fully packed for days and were ready to have all kinds of NYC adventures. I took different tacks. One day I tried to convince myself the real fun would be after the NYC trip when we had graduation and our Farewell Eighth Grade party. Another time I said it was actually a blessing I wasn't going on the trip because the babies might come early and I didn't want to miss that, did I?

But neither of these arguments held and I went

right back to thinking how long three days and two nights would feel, knowing that everyone was having fun on a vacation except for you.

I was especially dreading the moment when I'd have to tell Forrest. For a week now, he had told me he had some index cards he wanted to go over with me for our joint presentation to the Tomorrow's Leaders Today group. I kept putting him off, not wanting to imagine in detail any aspect of the trip I wouldn't be taking. The two of us onstage together was a strange but somehow lovely thought.

So it was with that kind of woe-is-me feeling that I shuffled to the auditorium for a special fortieth anniversary party for Principal Finklestein. I couldn't believe anyone could work anywhere that long, especially boring old Margaret Simon Middle School. We were "celebrating" with cupcakes followed by a live onstage interview. Bet would handle the interview and video it for a future *You Bet!* episode (yawn). I pictured Principal F. watching it over and over on his lonely evenings.

Giving out the anniversary cupcakes first was a big mistake. Someone had taken the time to write a "40" in icing on each one.

"Mmmm . . . *le petite gateau*," said Piper, downing hers and sharing the French word for cupcake.

The already excited eighth-grade class was now

sugar-buzzing on top of having "Field Trip-itis," as Ms. Russo had named it. Since the bus was leaving early Saturday morning, it was kind of like Field Trip Eve.

Shannon Andersen turned around and told us that Principal F.'s mother was there, in the auditorium, wearing a corsage and beaming in the front row. Bet started the interview with a photo montage of Principal F. through the years backed by a rousing instrumental track. It was the kind of music they might play before the start of the Super Bowl. I couldn't imagine how Bet had stood for this and guessed it was not her idea. Once the photos faded, the lights rose on the stage, where Bet and Principal F. were sitting in two living room chairs. It was like they were having this casual chat, a chat that happened to be occurring before a crowd of hundreds of students and teachers. None of us had any choice but to be there, in our seats, until the bell rang.

Bet's first questions were about his early aspirations.

"Well, Bet, it all started when I used to play school in our garden shed. I'd pretend I was the principal and my stuffed animals were the students."

Giggles rose up from the audience and teachers shushed them. The image of Principal F. instructing a class full of teddy bears and rag dolls filled the heads of the entire student body.

After the laughter died down, Bet reviewed his job

history, which never included any school other than Margaret Simon Middle School. He was very briefly a teacher, then an assistant vice principal, then a vice principal, and then principal. He nodded and smiled, occasionally tossing out a comment like, "That year, I created a blue-ribbon panel that shortened recess to allow more instructional time."

It was excruciating and then, suddenly, Bet took the wheel of the discussion. She made an unexpected U-turn back to 1973.

"Principal Finklestein, do you consider yourself an expert on Margaret Simon Middle School?"

"Why, yes, I do. I'd venture to say I know more about this school than any other living being," he said. "Hey, that reminds me of a funny story about the faculty parking lot . . ."

But Bet interrupted.

"So you know everything there is to know about Margaret Simon—or just stuff that happened while you were on the staff?"

"Oh, my dear, I know much more than that. I'm a student of history. Those who don't know their history are doomed to repeat it," Principal Finklestein said, nodding confidently at the audience.

"So you must know that the original Pink Locker Society—then called the Pink Locker Ladies—is a recognized club at this school?"

"What? I don't know about *recognized*. What does this have to do with my fortieth-anniversary party, Bet?"

Principal F. straightened himself up in his cozy brown chair.

"Well, you just said you're a student of school history, correct?"

"What is all this about? We haven't even covered the nineteen eighties yet."

Bet handed Principal F. a yellowed piece of paper that was curled at the edges.

"If you are familiar with the school's archived files, you'll recognize this document."

Principal F. put on his narrow reading glasses and looked over the document.

"What our principal is looking at is the original sanctioning paperwork for the Pink Locker Ladies. It's dated 1961."

"What is it?" people were murmuring in the audience. Piper reached down and grabbed my knee. I reached over and grabbed Kate's forearm. In a flash, our brains did the same little sashay. If this was the sanctioning document for the Pink Locker Ladies (aka the Pink Locker Society), then the PLS has *always* been a sanctioned group. And if that's true, then the very reason we were not allowed to go on the NYC trip was melting away like a popsicle in July.

"This document would have been in force in nineteen seventy-six, when the PLS was forced to shut down. And it would have remained in force through this school year when the Pink Locker Society made a long-overdue return to Margaret Simon Middle School," Bet said.

"Well, I would have to take a closer look at this, verify that it's not forged or being misinterpreted," Principal F. said

"But if it checks out, then the PLS is a sanctioned group and no one can be punished for being in it, right?"

"Well, technically that would be correct, but . . ."

"In fact, the sanctioning document would require Margaret Simon to offer this activity, right?" Bet said.

"I would have to consult the by-laws. It would probably depend on whether there was a teacher-advisor available to sponsor the group and several other technical details, details an eighth-grader—even one as bright as you, Bet—wouldn't be able to decipher."

"Agreed," Bet said. "Which is why I consulted the school board's attorney and she was able to verify everything I've said."

Principal F. adjusted himself in his seat and sat up straighter.

"Well, Ms. O'Connor knows her stuff, I suppose. Far be it from me to argue with the school board, some of whom are here today to celebrate my anniversary," Principal F. said, making a lame wave over to the right side of the auditorium.

The audience members were quieter now, not understanding exactly what was going on, but seeing that an eighth-grader had the principal on the ropes about something.

"Oh yes, right. We can continue this discussion off-line—and preferably before everyone departs for New York tomorrow," Bet said.

With just the mention of New York, cheers and whoops went up and the audience took on the manners of escaped farm animals.

"Um, excuse me. Hello? We're not done."

The crowd settled down only somewhat while Bet explained that we'd be ending the program with a song. She introduced the Margaret Simon Jazz Band and then led a rendition of "Happy Anniversary," sung to the tune of "Happy Birthday."

When it was over, Principal F. stood and bowed with his palms pressed together. The heavy velvet curtain closed and students jumped to their seats and headed for the exits.

"Did that just happen?" Piper said at a volume high enough to cause people three rows away to turn around.

"I think we are going to New York," Kate said.

"I don't know," I said, afraid to give into my barely contained joy.

"Well, here's how we find out for sure," Piper said. "To the principal's office! *Allons-y!*" (French for "Let's go!")

Twenty-five

We approached the front desk of the school office, but there was no one there to wait on us. We stood there, in total stillness, until we heard shreds of conversation coming from the principal's office. It was Principal F. and a female voice. I feared it was Bet, getting in major trouble. Maybe now *she* would be kept home from the New York trip, too? But soon we figured out the voice belonged to Mrs. Percy.

We didn't move a muscle and tried hard to decipher the *wa-womp-womp-womp* of it all. Occasionally, we could decipher a phrase but not the thread of what they were talking about.

"... after all these years ..."

"... without merit ..."

". . . once in a lifetime . . ."

". . . highlight of my career . . ."

Then the door opened and Principal F. stood and faced us.

"So you're here already. We were just going to call for you."

He motioned for us to join Mrs. Percy in his office. I found a seat and held on to both armrests. What could possibly happen next? I feared further punishment, an inquisition or an accusation that we had put Bet up to this.

"After considerable thought and the careful examination of new evidence, I am going to take back the penalty we had discussed," Principal F. said.

It was expressed in gobbledygook language, but the smile on Mrs. Percy's face said it all.

"And along with that, girls, the PLS can come into the light as an organization," she said.

"Yes, well, nineteen sixty-one was a full ten years before I arrived at Margaret Simon so I can hardly be held accountable for this . . . this record-keeping error," Principal F. said.

"Certainly not," Mrs. Percy said, and then gave us a wink.

"I didn't fully realize the scope of the work being done," Principal F. continued. "Or that the Tomorrow's Leaders Today committee planned to honor your group, and by extension"—he cleared his throat—"Margaret Simon Middle School."

"Lots to discuss, girls," Mrs. Percy said. "But the first order of business is that you need to go home and pack. Bus leaves at seven thirty tomorrow morning."

We made a move toward the door, but Principal F. stopped us.

"And Jemma," Principal F. said, "in your presentation to the Tomorrow's Leaders Today group, please acknowledge both me and the president of our school board in your opening remarks."

"Acknowledge you for what?" Piper said.

"For working through some difficult logistics so that the Pink Locker Society can continue its work and become a model for middle schools across the nation, and even the globe."

"But-but, you didn't help us at all," I said, surprised to hear what I was thinking come spilling out of my mouth.

"I would disagree. I verified that the sanctioning document is genuine, which clears the way for your future success. You literally couldn't have done it without me."

And before we could say any more, he said he had an important call to make, shuffled us out of his office, and closed the door.

Twenty-six

Woo-hoo! We needed to immediately tell our parents and start packing. And I needed to find Forrest and start working on our presentation. But at the very top of our to-do list was to find Bet and thank her. So immediately after school, the three of us walked over to her house. We linked arms and walked three astride down the sidewalk on that warm May afternoon. Forget the packing, forget the presentation, we had to find our girl! Funny that none of us even knew her before school had started in September. I had had no intention of making any new friends this year, but I had made a bunch.

I was even friendly with some seventh- and sixth-graders. Yes, they were younger, but I started to realize how the years make less of a difference the older you get. Clem's sister, Mimi, was a special friend—and a running buddy. Shannon Andersen, too, was popular in the same way Kate was, just for being friendly and easygoing with lots of people. She and I just "clicked," and I was sorry I'd be leaving her when I went off to high school.

But among all my new friends, Bet was at the top of the list. How many cups of tea had we shared at Lucky's? And how many hours had she listened to me analyze Forrest, and later, Jake? Many hours, too, I was a sounding board for her frustrations about boys and her run-ins with Principal F. over what she could report on for her *You Bet!* videocast.

"Bet!" we called out when she came out on the porch. Then we applauded and cheered her as if she had just hit a home run, which in a way she had.

"You guys are too much," she said, accepting our hugs.

We pulled her along with us to Main Street for celebratory ice cream cones. On the way, we asked her how she had unearthed the document. She explained that she requested and received permission from the school board to go through the archives.

"I said it was for a special school project. Four

days in a dusty back room, but it paid off," Bet said. "Not only did I find the PLS document, I found source documents for about ten other stories."

"But will you be able to broadcast any of them?" Kate asked. "I mean, the school year is almost over and Principal F. hasn't been too supportive."

"So true," Bet said. "But I've applied to Charter High School and they have a special journalism program, so I'm hoping I'll be able to do what I want, finally."

We ordered our cones—mint chocolate chip for me, mango for Piper, vanilla frozen yogurt for Kate, and chocolate truffle for Bet. Outside, we found an umbrella table and started talking—all at once—about New York City. Though we were plenty loud, anyone passing by would have had the same trouble we did, just hours ago, when we heard only fragments from behind the closed door of the principal's office.

"*Breakfast at Tiffany's* . . ."

"Top of the Rock . . ."

". . . One hundred and two stories high . . ."

"Trip of a lifetime . . ."

Back at home, we pledged to not text each other for at least an hour so we could pack and prepare. Mrs. Percy had already called my parents with the good news. I walked in my room to find my suitcase with wheels and stacks of fresh laundry waiting to be packed. The clothing issue kept me up half the night. I needed a comfortable—yet stylish—outfit for the bus ride there. Then I needed something more professional-looking for our Tomorrow's Leaders Today conference. And finally, to fill in, I had to pack a bunch of city-ready clothes for all the sightseeing we'd be doing.

"Don't overpack, Jemma. You always do," my mother bellowed from outside my closed room door.

Just a few nights before, I had helped her pack her own suitcase for the hospital.

"I have to be ready at a moment's notice now," she had said.

I almost cried—tears of sadness, happiness, both?—when I saw her carefully tuck in two little come-home-from-the-hospital outfits. Both had yellow ducks on them since we still didn't know whether I was getting brothers, sisters, or one of each. This was really happening, though. Very soon, I'd be a big sister.

"You have to text me if anything happens," I ordered my dad.

"I will, Jem. But your mom's not due for a few more weeks," he said.

New York. Graduation. Two new siblings. It was a lot to handle in such a short time. I packed until the wee hours. When I was finally done, I couldn't have stuffed another item, even the thinnest sock, into my suitcase. I didn't realize until we were on the bus, pointed toward New York, that I hadn't packed any period supplies of any kind.

Twenty-seven

Waiting in line to board the bus, some people chatted up a storm. Others cocooned themselves into their iPods, an attempt to look cool and deal with being overtired. Me? I ping-ponged between two boys. First off, I had to confront the Jake situation. He brightened in a way that nearly broke my heart when he saw me through the glass of his window seat.

"Jemma! I thought you couldn't go?" Jake said out the open bus window.

"It got all worked out," I said, and smiled.

"Excellent," he said. "I'll save you a seat."

"Um, no. Don't, Jake. I, um, already promised Kate."

"Okay, well, I'll come and say hi when you get on."

I nodded and started to think of the uncomfortable conversation ahead of me/us. I was just about to lean confidentially in and tell Kate what I was about to do, when someone tapped my shoulder.

"Jemma! Where've you been?" Forrest asked.

"I'm here," I said.

"We have got to do that presentation thing. I mean, I have index cards, but I think we're supposed to talk for fifteen minutes."

"Yeah, we should probably have some visuals, too. Slides."

"We'll have to do it tonight—at the hotel. I guess," he said.

"Right. It'll be fine. It's not till tomorrow. I have my laptop."

"Cool," Forrest said. "Where are you sitting on the bus? Want me to save you and Kate a seat?"

"Sure, that'd be great."

Once boarded, with all our luggage stored and tagged, I felt like I could fall asleep and stay asleep until the city skyline was in view. Instead, I gathered my courage and walked down the narrow bus aisle to where Jake was sitting, a Yankees cap perched on his head.

"Hey," he said.

We arranged for some seat switching so I could sit down next to him.

"Hey," he said again, once we were all arranged.

I stared at the green vinyl seat in front of me, wondering how anyone begins a conversation like this. I knew he'd be upset, yet I felt so honestly that it had nothing to do with him. That is, he didn't do anything wrong and there was nothing wrong with him. In fact, there was a lot right with him. But, bottom line, I knew I should like him more—and in that way—if I was going to be his girlfriend. Call it chemistry, a spark. But whatever you call it, I didn't "have it" for Jake.

"You are such a nice guy, Jake. Such a good friend," I began.

"You're breaking up with me, aren't you?" he said. "Right here, right now."

"I'm sorry," I said, and started to cry.

"Why are you crying? I'm the one who's getting dumped."

"I'm just sad 'cause I know how it feels," I said.

"Yeah, okay. Don't cry. People are looking," Jake said.

I wiped my face with the back of my hand.

"Honestly, Jake. I don't know what I am doing half the time."

"I know," Jake said. "It's cute."

"See what I mean? You were mad for half a second and you're right back to being nice again."

Jake sat back in his seat and smiled, but not exactly happily, at the seat back in front of us both.

"I could list, like, five girls who like you, you know," I said.

"That doesn't help, but thanks," Jake said.

And with that I stood up and stumble-bumbled back to my seat. I gave Kate the recap and quickly fell asleep leaning against her shoulder.

Twenty-eight

Kate let me sleep until the bus stopped in front of our hotel. She gently shook my shoulder and I emerged from my sleepy fog.

"We're here, Jem," Kate said.

Almost everyone else was up and gathering their things. I did the same. Kate handed me my purse and I stepped down the bus steps onto the hotel's curved driveway. We filed inside through an enormous revolving door. The hotel lobby seemed like an airport concourse, with just as many comings and goings. People checking in, luggage carts whizzing by, three restaurants within view, escalators going up, and three different banks of elevators. The hotel was so huge that it wasn't like there was one elevator that went to every floor. There were fifteen elevators and they all served different floors. You had to pick the right one.

Ms. Russo stood in the lobby with a MARGARET SIMON MIDDLE SCHOOL sign attached to a tall pole. We all gathered around and Mr. Ford used a bullhorn to direct us to the next step—getting our room keys and getting settled in. Then after lunch we were going to the Statue of Liberty and the Lower East Side Tenement Museum, followed by dinner in Chinatown. The nighttime hours were "on your own," but that meant on your own along with your chaperone— one adult for every four students.

The throng of us ran for the escalators and elevators as soon as we were dismissed. Hurray for us, we got on the right elevators—the one for floors 18–26. It zipped us up to the twenty-first floor so fast that my ears popped. Trailed by our chaperone, Mrs. Pinsky (and her zebra-striped luggage), we found our room down a long hallway. We had scored the ultimate in field-trip luck. Our request that we all be together was granted and our fourth member was Bet.

We had two rooms, with a door that linked them. The rooms were sleek and modern, not unlike the decor in our Pink Locker Society office. But they were also compact and space-efficient. A curved desk fit just-so near the window, and the two beds were high and thick with fluffy white bedding. The bathroom was modern with a tall curving faucet for the sink and outfitted with organic fig shampoo and cherry blossom soap.

"*J'adore* the view!" said Piper as she flung the curtains open a little wider on Fifty-third Street below. "Mom, what's the French word for view?" Piper asked.

"*La vue*, I think," said Mrs. Pinsky. She had set her zebra suitcase up on the luggage rack and was now browsing the hotel's spa menu.

I wished that my bedroom window back home opened up to a view like this. Everything about New York was bigger and more fascinating than anywhere else, especially home. If you haven't been there, go as quickly as you can! And yes, it is as unbelievable as it looks on TV. If I lived in New York City, I'd never, ever get bored. How could you?

I guess the nap on the bus had done me good. I was sad about Jake—sad because I knew I hurt his feelings. But I was also majorly relieved that I had taken care of that unfinished business. It was beyond good to see so many new things. There was no end to the distractions—people, buildings, taxicabs, street vendors, different smells, and store windows. For at least an hour, I completely forgot about my mom back home about to have twins. When I texted her, she answered right back: *still pregnant, have fun.*

As our group walked to find some lunch—pizza, of course—I couldn't help but daydream. What would life would be like if I moved to New York City and went to high school there? There was something about the place that just begged you to leave everything behind and start fresh, become a New Yorker. Which—funnily enough—was the theme of the afternoon.

You can start no fresher than to be an immigrant, leaving your country in, say, 1900, and coming through Ellis Island. I should have brought a jacket for the boat ride, which chilled us but provided an excellent view of the New York City skyline. And perhaps I should have worn more comfortable shoes, not strappy sandals, for the climb up, up, up into the Statue of Liberty. We took photos from every conceivable angle: from high up in the crown, looking down, to lying down on the grass beneath Lady Liberty. It was very hard to get her—head to foot—in the shot. The more we cut off her head or cut her off at the knees, the more uproariously we laughed.

The boat ride also gave us lots of time to talk about the PLS. We went down below and sat at a table with Ms. Russo.

"Seems too bad that just when the PLS is recognized, we have to move on and graduate," Kate said.

"Don't see it that way," Ms. Russo said. "Be proud

of the work you did and how you got the PLS to this point."

"Mrs. Percy said something about announcing us at graduation. Is that going to happen?" Piper asked.

"That'd be too weird," I said.

"Would it?" Ms. Russo asked. "Because I think it would be fitting for you to be recognized. Perhaps you can introduce next year's Pink Locker Society members, too."

"People can't know who we are," I said.

"Even though there's not much time left, that could be a pain, actually," Piper said. "If people knew who we were, they'd be bugging us and everyone would want to see the office."

"True. But maybe there's some middle ground?" Ms. Russo said. "Think about it."

"We will," I said. "And I guess we have to finalize our replacements."

"Yes, I'd get on that ASAP," Ms. Russo said. "And are you all set for tomorrow—for your presentation with Forrest at the Tomorrow's Leaders Today conference?"

"Just about," I said. This was like saying "I'm almost there," when I hadn't even left my house.

Enough stalling, I thought. Time to find Forrest and make a plan.

Twenty-nine

I surveyed the entire ferry looking for Forrest. I would have texted, but our teachers had the brilliant idea that we couldn't use our phones (except to take photos) during the entire field trip.

"Be where you are, people," Ms. Russo said. "Experience New York, not your cell phone."

That was all well and good, but now I was experiencing New York in a bit of a panic. Shortly, we'd be at a museum and then we'd be dining in Chinatown. After that, I knew it would be late. I had left approximately no time for Forrest and me to work on this presentation.

"If you wouldn't have volunteered to work with

Forrest, you wouldn't have gotten stuck making this big presentation," Piper said with a wink.

True enough. Kate offered to help, but it was one of those times when it was easier just to do it yourself than to involve a lot of people. I didn't want to involve Forrest, either. But we were stuck doing a joint presentation because the Tomorrow's Leaders Today organizers had insisted our talk be relevant to both girls and boys. On the agenda they sent, it was titled "Pink Locker, Blue Locker: Peer-to-Peer Intervention for Middle Grade Students."

I still didn't know what to expect from the Tomorrow's Leaders Today conference. The only people I had known to go to this conference were eighth-graders in overdrive. You know the ones—they've won every conceivable local award and scholarship. Many are their newspaper clippings. Their parents are likely to be super-duper-involved in their lives. Sometimes, they are immensely talented in science or already know how to speak Russian. Perhaps they've identified a need in the community—say, warm pajamas for needy kids—and they've mounted a drive to correct this problem straightaway.

Adults love these students, who are on a straight road toward whatever university or life path they'd like to select. I think of them as grown-ups disguised as eighth-graders. It wasn't that I didn't like these people—I mean, technically, Bet was in this category. It's just that I couldn't understand how they had figured out their life's passion so quickly. I was just Jemma and, let's face it, I had stumbled into the Pink Locker Society.

Fortunately, I also stumbled into Forrest when we were filing into the Chinese restaurant. It was ablaze with red lanterns and pink tablecloths and smelled nothing short of heavenly to weary, hungry travelers.

"After we get back to the hotel, we've gotta do this," he said.

"Yes. Perfect. Meet you in the lobby."

And then he was gone again. Mrs. Pinsky gathered our group and pointed us toward Ms. Russo's table, where she was already pouring us warm cups of tea. Weirdly, Piper was not at our table.

"I saw her on the bus. She must be here somewhere," Kate said.

We scanned the restaurant for her and came up empty, until Kate pointed her out across the room. She was sitting next to Forrest, who was sitting next to Taylor. Piper and Forrest seemed to be talking conspiratorially, as if they didn't want Taylor to hear.

So, this meant only one of two possible things:

1. Piper and Forrest were getting back together.
2. Taylor and Forrest were getting back together. Remember how protective he was about the bullying?

I looked down at my wrist for my soda tab bracelet. It wasn't there. I had left it behind like more than a few other things I forgot at home (my straightening iron and my lip balm, to name just two). OK, I thought, I don't need the bracelet to remind me of my five goals: being a good friend, becoming a good big sister, running, the PLS, and stopping the whole Forrest thing.

In these last months, I had succeeded at almost all of them, almost all of the time. I decided not to give up. I turned my attention from Forrest to my tall Chinese menu, which served as an excellent screen between me and the rest of the restaurant. I immersed myself in its pages, its multiple sections and sometimes-confusing descriptions of the dishes.

There were twelve soups listed, including shark's fin. Should I stick with something traditional, like kung pao shrimp, or go out of my comfort zone and try pig's belly with preserved mustard greens? There was always whole fish, Hunan style. Or maybe I'd ask the waitress to explain the difference between Double Delight, Triple Delight, and Double Winter Delight.

I also considered how I'd enjoy the shock value of ordering boneless duck feet with black bean sauce. But I was hungry and I couldn't imagine boneless duck feet being very filling.

Just as I was settling on chicken with ginger and scallions, Piper returned to our table.

"What's everyone ordering?" she asked.

"I'm getting the vegetable lo mein," Kate said.

"Where'd you go?" Mrs. Pinsky asked.

"Um, I had to talk to someone. About something," Piper said.

"Well, that's nice and vague. What are you getting? The waitress will be right over," Mrs. Pinsky said.

"I don't even need to look. I'm getting the orange chicken."

I didn't chime in with what I was planning to order. In truth, I was pouting, but no one noticed. The restaurant was noisy, our table was large, and there were lots of other talkers. Bet, for instance, was deep in conversation with Ms. Russo about *You Bet!*

"All I'm saying is, if the PLS is a recognized club, why can't I show the episodes that Principal F. wouldn't let me broadcast before? I think I should be allowed to do it before school lets out."

Of course, Ms. Russo agreed that she should be able to.

"Principal Finklestein has been giving in on a lot of issues this week. I'm just not sure you're going to convince him on that one," Ms. Russo said.

Thirty

Back at the hotel, the adults wanted us in pajamas with heads on pillows by eleven. But we sensed the tiredness of our chaperones; it was like a window of freedom opening. There was talk of watching movies, finding the hotel's game room, and, for the truly fired up, the swimming pool. But Forrest and I had homework to do. I started to resent this whole conference and how it was going to force us to miss the Empire State Building and the tour of Radio City Music Hall.

"I can't believe we have to do work right now," I said when Forrest found me in the lobby.

"Sucks, right? Maybe it won't take that long," he said.

I had started making some notes on the back of a Statue of Liberty pamphlet, but it wasn't much. We walked toward the elevators and I remembered that I needed to get the laptop from my room. Forrest pressed the up button and shoved his hands into the pockets of his army-green shorts. He looked nervous, which was a switch because it was usually me who was all weird around him.

"I, uh, have something to say to you, Jemma," he said.

I turned to him and the elevator doors opened.

"Hold up!" Luke Zubin yelled from across the lobby.

With him, about half of the Margaret Simon baseball team crashed toward us and joined us in the mirrored elevator.

"We're going swimming, McCann. You comin'?"

"Can't," Forrest said.

"Uh-huh," Luke said, raising his eyebrows in a suggestive way.

Was this a reference in some way to Piper, or Taylor? Or even both of them? I instantly guessed that what Forrest was about to tell me had something to do with one of them. Just great.

A handful of the team got out on seventeen, but the rest were apparently with us all the way to twenty-one. When it was my floor, I said I could handle it and just meet him in the lounge—a kind of living room we had scouted earlier in the day.

"It's all right. I'll come with you," he said.

"Okay."

The hallway was clear, but he didn't say anything more. I knocked on the door, got my computer, and told Mrs. Pinsky where I'd be.

"Good for you, Jemma. The rest of them are just goofing off tonight," she said.

Oh, how I wished I could also be goofing off. Aside from the awkwardness with Forrest, I didn't know if I could focus my mind on the task. Something about New York left me so overstimulated that my brain just wanted to shut down for the night. A swim and a movie sounded perfect.

Forrest and I were not alone in the lounge, a cozy space with soft red couches, TVs, and an elegant glass water dispenser with a silver spigot. Inside, slices of lemon and lime floated in the chilled water. Bet was there, shooting video of some chorus members singing an old song about New York and how if you could make it there, you could make it anywhere. Nearby, an intense game of Nerf basketball was just getting started. Not a grown-up in sight.

"Let's play H-O-R-S-E," Tyler Lima told a couch full of basketball players.

"This doesn't look like a very good spot," I said.

"It's amazing, actually," Forrest said.

"Not for getting work done."

"No, but in general," Forrest said.

"We have to find someplace quiet or we're doomed," I said.

"I know a place," Forrest said, and led me back to the elevators.

"Not again. Now where to?"

He pressed the up button and again plunged his hands in his pockets. Was he really that nervous to tell me about his latest girlfriend? The elevator doors closed but the car hadn't moved.

"I can handle it, you know. Just get it out and let's get it over with," I said.

He started to say something but the elevator stopped and the doors opened to reveal Ms. Russo and Mr. Ford. Their New Year's Eve wedding had been so romantic and I still thought of them as newlyweds.

"Good evening, kids. Having fun?"

"Yeah," I said unconvincingly.

"We're going out for a late-night stroll," they said as the doors closed.

"Then why are you going up?" Forrest said.

"We're not," Mr. Ford said. "You must have gotten on the wrong elevator."

As we went down twenty floors, I felt myself losing what little grip I had.

"Oh, great," I said.

"Don't panic. I know a quiet place. For real," Forrest said.

He led me to a bank of elevators I hadn't seen before. We entered the skyward car and took it to the very top of the hotel, the thirty-second floor. The doors opened and we were much more alone than before. We walked through glass doors and found ourselves outside. The view of the city took my breath away. It wasn't like I hadn't been to big cities before this trip. I had, but this was different. My brain just couldn't quite absorb all those buildings and all those people and all those lives going on in every window and taxicab. As I got hold of myself, there was more to bombard my senses. On the deck, candles illuminated umbrella tables and chaise lounges around a rooftop pool.

"Zubin's looking for the pool, but you can't get up here unless you know where the special elevator is," Forrest said.

"I don't know how anyone gets anything done in this city," I said.

"I guess you get used to it. Like anyplace," Forrest said.

I thought about confronting him again to tell me whatever had to be said. But I felt like I needed to reserve my energy. We sat at a table set apart from the handful of other couples, and I opened my lap-top.

"So, I forgot my index cards, but I can tell you what I was going to say."

I nodded.

"I'm supposed to talk about the Blue Locker Society as a pilot program. And I can say that it was good."

"What happened?"

"We had meetings. On the school roof, which was not nearly so cool as this one."

"Did you answer questions?"

"Um, yeah. Sort of. I mean, guys don't have questions like girls do."

"A long time ago, you told me they did."

Stupid, stupid. Why do I always reveal to Forrest that I remember every word we'd ever exchanged?

"Okay. That's not what I meant," Forrest said. "Guys don't want to talk about stuff. They keep things to themselves, you know?"

I knew a little too well.

"So you took no questions and you answered no questions. What did you do on the roof?" I asked.

"Played trash-can basketball, mostly."

It was tempting to just flip out, but I had to laugh. The Pink Locker Society had answered more than two hundred questions and the Blue Locker Society had answered exactly zero. Maybe it was the exhaustion but I did start to laugh.

"What?" Forrest said.

"That," I said between laughing, "is going to make for an impressive presentation tomorrow."

He laughed a little, too, and said, "Well, it's your show for the most part, right?"

"I guess it will have to be. You just stand there and look good," I said.

And then, again, I had massive regret for how my mouth gets ahead of my brain sometimes. Did I really just suggest to Forrest that I think he looks good? Perhaps I should dive into the pool, clothes and all, just to change the subject.

"I do have something to tell you, Jem. Nothing related to this thing tomorrow."

OK. Go. Go. Just say it already.

"I'm—I'm sorry . . ."

Bad news, just as I expected.

"Sorry for what?"

"Sorry that I . . . put you in that spot. Asked you to, you know, be my fake girlfriend."

Oh, that. Why was he apologizing now? I had broken up with him. That moment had been impossible to forget.

"Okay," I said. "I'm not mad at you."

"I know. I just see now that—that it wasn't fair. It wasn't a fair thing to ask."

"It all worked out, right?" I said. "We're friends."

"Yeah," Forrest said. "And you ended up going out with Jake, who's liked you since fourth grade or whatever."

Oh, Jake. Now I felt even worse. Fourth grade!

It wasn't as bad as me liking Forrest since preschool, but still. I thought about correcting him, telling him Jake and I broke up. But I wanted to let him keep going, see where this was headed.

"So that's what I wanted to say," Forrest said.

I was happy to switch topics to the presentation and my PowerPoint slides. I quickly threw together some basics ones, explaining how the PLS started, how many questions we had answered, and how many girls we had helped. Forrest seemed interested and made a few suggestions. Thirty minutes later, I felt prepared enough and told Forrest we'd better go.

"Really? I don't want to go," he said. "Zubin's going to find this pool and then it's going to be all cannon-balls and squirt guns."

"Fine, let's stay a few more minutes, but I'm about to fall asleep right here in this spot."

We turned our chairs to face the twinkling sky-line. Once we stopped talking, we could listen to the other small parties chatter. Then we watched a family with two toddlers go for a late swim. I thought of my mom when I saw the little ones, and all that awaited me at home. But mostly I thought about how New York was so very full of surprises. Just forty-eight hours ago, I thought I wouldn't be taking this trip at all. And somehow, I was in New York sitting atop a glamorous hotel with none other than Forrest McCann.

Thirty-one

The hotel's wake-up call came over the telephone and sounded like someone playing the xylophone. *Zing-zong-zing-zing.* It was soft and unalarming, yet it was such an unusual sound that it woke me instantly. Lying in a heap of luxurious sheets and blankets, I had that moment where you don't remember where you are or what you're supposed to be doing. Then it all came rushing back at once and I started checking things off the to-do list in my head. Shower, personal grooming, find the laptop, wake Bet and Kate. Piper said I could wake her, too, but she was a bear without sleep so I just let her and her mom keep right on snoozing. Bet could show them the video later.

I put on my presentation outfit, carefully assembled

back at home with help from my mom and Bet. Bet, I figured, had onstage experience and could tell me a thing or two. I slipped on my cream skirt, a light-weight navy sweater, and pearls. It looked professional without making me look too old, or like a sailor. I briefly considered wearing something pink, but it seemed way too cute. I slipped my feet into my navy flats and we were off.

Ms. Russo was already down at the cab stand, but we had to wait for Forrest. I imagined him deeply asleep after last night's hotel-wide adventures that included swimming, elevator races, and eating left-over Chinese food on the roof. I held an orange juice in one hand and my laptop in the other while Bet put the finishing touches on my makeup. I didn't wear much makeup usually, but for the occasion, I decided to use some shimmery eye shadow for the first time. I closed my eyes to be a better makeover candidate.

"You're done," she said.

When I opened my eyes, there he was. His hair was a little bit everywhere and he wore rumpled kha-kis, an equally rumpled blue button-down, and a tie that was . . . pink. It felt like a sort of tribute, as if he had brought me a pink rose.

"Nice tie, Forrest," Ms. Russo said.

The convention center registration area was filled with other eighth-graders, all waiting to receive their name tags and fat folders of information about the day's events. Some were lugging what looked like science experiments. Others were tapping away on laptops. Immediately, I felt like the person who had not studied enough for the test.

"Ten minutes until you're on," Ms. Russo said, leading us through a winding series of crowded hallways and ballrooms. Finally, we found the SPEAKERS ONLY door and walked together down a long, sloping corridor. We were at stage level and a woman with a STAFF T-shirt was waiting for us like the hostess at the entrance of a restaurant.

"Colwin and McCann?" she asked.

Forrest and I looked at each other, reacting to the odd sound of our names mashed together like that.

"Yes," Ms. Russo answered for us.

The hostess passed us on to another staff person who led us up to the stage, but just close enough so we could see the seats filling up and no one could see us yet. The room looked large enough to host a royal wedding.

"You'll be introduced. Then walk to the podium and turn on the microphone. Little red button," the stagehand told us. "Here's your clicker for the Power-Point."

Now, with no way to escape, my heart was beating fast.

"Why did I agree to this?" I asked Ms. Russo, some panic in my voice.

"Because you'll do a great job telling the world about the Pink Locker Society," she said.

"But I don't even like oral report day in English— and that's in front of only twenty-five people."

I saw Bet's smile behind her video camera. Then the stagehand shooed away Bet, Kate, and Ms. Russo to their seats. He attached a tiny microphone to Forrest's jacket lapel and told me I could use the one attached to the podium. Forrest and I stood alone, waiting for the call. The audience hushed. We could hear the emcee giving instructions about how people should move all the way over in their rows.

"We have people standing in back," he said. "This is a sold-out show."

"Great," I said, gripping my note cards tightly.

Standing in the dark, Forrest leaned down and whispered in my ear. "Don't worry. You'll be great."

Before I could react to his soft words in my ear, we heard, "Let's welcome Jemma Colwin and Forrest McCann."

We walked together across the stage. I kept my eyes focused on the podium, our destination and where I would find the all-important red button for the microphone. Only once I located it and clicked it on did I lift my head to take in the full audience, from east to west and north to south. It was an ocean of people.

"Hello and thank you so much for having us," I said, my voice trembling like an instrument I was just learning to play.

I wondered how I'd ever be able to get through a dozen slides. I should have set my alarm extra early and gone for a run to calm my nerves. Then an idea hit me. The Pink Locker Society is about being honest and asking for help. I could, right at this moment, do exactly that.

"Has anyone here ever been really nervous?"

A big show of hands, including Forrest, who was not expecting this audience participation segment.

"Well, the truth is, I'm really nervous right now. And it helps me to know that you have had times like that, too. The Pink Locker Society is an advice-giving Web site for girls, a safe place where people can admit stuff about themselves and get help. So I'm standing here thinking: What would we say to someone like me if she wrote in to say she was nervous about making a big presentation?"

I set down my note cards and my PowerPoint clicker.

"I think we'd say, number one, be prepared, which I am. Sort of. I prepared by spending this entire school year reading hundreds of questions sent in by girls, and boys, at my school."

There were some giggles when I said boys had written in, too.

"Yes, boys do write in to the PLS. Forrest will talk about boys in a minute. But I can tell you that they wanted to know some of the same stuff girls want to know: How do I know if my crush likes me? And am I normal?"

The room was quiet and I no longer felt as fidgety. I moved back to the podium and stepped through my note cards and slides. I saw people taking notes as I explained the process we went through to train ourselves, set up the Web site, and begin taking questions from the girls at Margaret Simon Middle School.

"We specialize in the PBBs—periods, bras, and boys," I said, and clicked on a slide that explained it in bold type.

The audience laughed and nudged each other.

"It's okay to laugh. I'm used to it. But these body changes—and let me just say it's not just girls who are going through body changes in middle school—are one hundred percent normal. It happens to all of us, so should everyone be worried and frightened about it?"

"She's right," I heard Forrest say.

He had turned on his microphone and I accepted that as my cue to let him talk about the very early steps of the Blue Locker Society.

"Okay, so we tried a Blue Locker Society and it

wasn't perfect," Forrest said. "Boys—well, speaking for myself—I don't want to talk this whole thing to death. I also felt weird asking guys to be in the Blue Locker Society, to be honest. But guys like to play trash-can basketball, so I created a trash-can basketball league."

I had been enjoying not speaking, but suddenly my heart rate sped up and I felt sweat on my palms. Forrest hadn't told me it was an actual league. *Was he really going to talk to Tomorrow's Leaders Today about trash-can basketball?*

"We have a sweet location up on our school roof," Forrest said, and showed his own PowerPoint slide of the gravelly school roof.

OMG, he is really going to crash and burn here. We are supposed to be talking about helping other people get through middle school and puberty!

"But I made a requirement of anyone who wanted to play with us up on the roof. Eighth-graders had to bring a sixth-grader or a seventh-grader with them. So we weren't solving hundreds of problems directly like Jemma and her crew, but it was, like, a good deed for the older guys. You have to hang out with younger guys at school, get to know them."

Forrest flashed to a slide showing a mix of upper- and lowerclassmen on the roof together.

"It's not our only problem, but guys want to have

a group of friends and feel, you know, cool. And this was a way to do that for sixth- and seventh-graders, too. We just upgraded to a Nerf hoop and we're picking seventh-graders who will take over the club next year. Any questions?" Forrest said, handing the clicker back to me.

I was nearly speechless, except that we had to answer audience questions and there were many. The guys in the audience—so typical!—didn't ask too many, but Forrest got a few. There were loads for me from girls:

How do you start a Pink Locker Society?
Where do you meet?
How many girls do you need?
What if you don't give good advice?
How do you set up a Web site?
Would it look good to have something like this on a college application?

One dark-haired girl wearing a sequined beret stood up from the audience.

"You guys are so awesome," she said. "I can't even imagine all the people you have helped. You're like middle-school guardian angels."

"Oh, I don't know about that," I said. "It's just basic advice. Anyone can do it. That's why we're here."

"She just doesn't want to brag," Forrest said. "The PLS is amazing and not everyone would be this good at it. I know for a fact that Jemma helped someone who was being bullied. She confronted the bully herself. And another time, she saved her friend's life, who was choking."

People applauded, and I felt my face redden. I nervously tucked my hair behind my ear. Suddenly I felt so drained. We had done it. Made the trip, made the presentation. I felt entirely out of answers.

Just in time, the emcee thanked us and told the group that we were nominated to speak at the international Tomorrow's Leaders Today conference. There was a little more applause and then he said the next session would be starting in ten minutes. I removed my name-tag necklace and felt officially off duty.

"That was wonderful, Jemma. And you, too, Forrest," Ms. Russo said. "People are asking if you'll do speaking engagements at their schools."

"That's amazing. You're a star, Jemma," Kate said.

Bet hadn't turned her camera off since we hit the stage. I smiled at her. Doing another presentation was not something I wanted to think about right then. I looked in Bet's camera lens and was relieved to finally say, "That's a wrap."

Thirty-two

Back at the hotel, there was a bouquet of pink flowers waiting for us at the lobby desk. Piper, looking well-rested, was waiting, too.

"They're from Principal Finklestein," she said. "He says congratulations and to expect to be recognized during the awards ceremony at graduation."

I rolled my eyes and Kate laughed.

"Jemma was great, Piper. You should have seen her."

"I heard. Forrest texted me," Piper said.

"I think I need a nap," I said.

"That's fine," Ms. Russo said. "Why don't you rejoin the group at two, when we're going to the Metropolitan Museum of Art."

"And Central Park," Kate said.

I took myself upstairs, ate a bagel Mrs. Pinsky left for me, and fell deeply asleep. When I woke up, I felt refreshed and sooooooo glad that our presentation was finally over. But when I looked in the mirror, I was a bit rumpled. I shouldn't have slept in my fancy clothes. I switched from the cream skirt to jeans. I left on the pearls because it seemed like a classy New York thing to do.

When a place's slogan is "5,000 years of art," you know you are not going to see even half of it in a single afternoon. Mrs. Pinsky said Piper, Kate, Bet, and I could be on our own at the museum, so we made it a scavenger hunt. We'd visit just a handful of artworks but really good ones. My mom asked me to visit her favorite painting, *Juan de Pareja*, by Velásquez. Bet wanted to see all the armor. Mrs. Pinsky recommended the exhibit on important women photographers.

"Let's not forget the gift store," Piper said.

"Agreed," said Kate.

We moved swiftly up staircases, elevators, and escalators. We were often lost, but if you're going to be lost, you couldn't ask for more interesting scenery. We bumped into thousand-year-old pottery and antique ballgowns before we found *Juan de Pareja*. He stared out at us, dignified, from somewhere in the sixteen hundreds. Next, we found the armor and ghostly knights on horseback.

"Let's talk knights in shining armor, Jem," Piper said. "What's up with you and McCann?"

"Nothing," I said a little too quickly. On the one hand, our presentation was over, so the only reason for us to spend time together was over. On the other hand . . .

"It's not nothing. He so likes you," Piper said.

"I think so, too," Kate said.

"Maybe he likes *you*, Piper," I said.

"Me? That was a one-time thing, believe me," Piper said. "Not that I think he's bad news or anything."

"He was very complimentary of Jemma at the Tomorrow's Leaders Today conference," Bet said.

I admit to replaying our morning together, but now I wished everyone would stop talking about him/me/us. I wished I had packed my soda tab bracelet. It was a silly thing, but it helped me. Did I have the strength to withstand this? It was a smart goal to stop obsessing about a boy who clearly didn't like me, but what if he actually did? In that case, I didn't know what my goal should be.

"Let's go to the Temple of Dendur," I said, and linked arms with Bet.

We strode across miles of gallery floor until we

were there. It was not hard to find, as it was enormous and a top attraction for which there were signs. Being inside an Egyptian temple from 15 BC helped me escape from myself. We stopped beside the reflecting pool, listened half-heartedly to a nearby tour guide, and realized we were already late for our meet-up with Mrs. Pinsky.

Trying to find the museum exit proved the toughest scavenger hunt of all. Galleries turned into other galleries, from Byzantine art to the American section, with its full facade of a colonial home. We moved through the armor, endless ancient sculptures, chalices, and shards of pottery, but we still hadn't found the way out. We had wound our way back to the temple and our hearts felt low. New York could wear a person out. My brain refused to accept any more new information. I thought of home and its simple floor plan, how easy it was to find my way.

"Stay put," Mrs. Pinsky texted us, and came to the rescue.

She ushered us to the main entrance, where we walked down steep steps and on toward Central Park. I felt homesick, I guess, but the expanse of nature did my head good. Spring had come to the park, with green grass and lush leaves on the trees. We walked downhill in this canyon of the city as evening closed in. We met up with the rest of our group, lined up for burgers and shakes at an outdoor stand, and ate in the evening twilight under white festival lights. The mood at our long table turned sentimental, with talk of next year, which would bring different high schools and sad farewells.

Kate, Bet, and I had applied to Charter, but we didn't know if we got in. Piper was going to Cedar Cliff High School. Of course, you could still be friends with people even if you didn't go to the same school. It's not like one of us was moving. As part of my pact with myself, I hadn't asked Forrest where he'd be going to high school.

I took the last noisy sip of my shake and surveyed the outdoor dining room, eyeing the Margaret Simon Middle School Class of 2011. Everyone seemed to laugh a little harder than usual at each other's jokes, and draped arms around each other more than we had to. Walking back to the hotel, I didn't know if I should be sad for what was ending or happy for what was to come.

Thirty-three

Before we boarded the bus, I made a last check-in with Mom. It yielded no news. She was still waiting, the twins apparently in no hurry to be born. I gave Kate the report and we checked our luggage in the cargo hold. Unlike my in-bound trip, I was determined to stay awake for the ride home. We found seats about midway, not directly in front of Forrest but not that far from him, either. Mrs. Pinsky sat up front with some of the other worn-out chaperones. Ms. Russo positioned herself near the four of us.

"Girls, I think we've got to talk about next steps," she said.

She meant the next generation of the Pink Locker Society, a topic that was oh-so-bittersweet. It was in the same category as the imminent farewells to our friends. It signaled the end. I kept feeling guilty that we weren't answering any questions while we were in New York, but there was really no way. Ms. Russo said, in addition to picking new girls, we should choose a date that we'd stop answering questions for the school year and let our readers know.

"We nominated Mimi Caritas," I said.

"And Shannon Andersen," Piper said.

"That's only two," Kate said. "Who else?"

"We should have three at a minimum. Four is even better," Ms. Russo said.

"These girls are going to absolutely pass out when they hear they have been picked. It would make an excellent documentary-style show," Bet said.

"Except I'm not sure everyone should know who they are," I said.

"Agreed," Piper said.

"Hey, look," I said, pointing out the faraway New York City skyline as we sped down the highway.

The bus had just crossed a giant bridge. It felt a little like a spell had been broken.

"*Au revoir*, New York," Piper said.

The trip was a sort of dream that had ended, and it was back to real life. On top of everything, or maybe because of everything, my stomach hadn't felt right all morning. I excused myself and went to the bathroom in the back of the bus. It was a long walk there past a million people, including Forrest. The bus lurched and I had to regain my balance like a sailor on a ship. I kept on going and passed by Taylor. She pulled on my arm.

"Stop by when you're on your way back to your seat," she said.

Even though I'd helped her, we were not super-friendly. So I wondered what she had to say and I wanted to know if it had something to do with her and Forrest. Every time I let myself think he might like me (as everyone was saying), I remembered how he was so worried about Taylor and her bullying problem. I checked that the narrow bathroom door was marked "vacant" and went inside. The bathroom was less insulated than the rest of the bus and it felt closer to the outside, and certainly louder. So for the first thirty seconds, I was thinking about the noise and how I didn't want to be in there for too long. But then everything changed. Yes, my life changed in a coach bus bathroom.

I spotted a smudge of something reddish-brown on my underwear. The stain had ever so slightly leaked through my jeans. It was by no means a large stain, but it was there, red and unmistakable. So I had the thrill and delight of finally, finally, FINALLY getting my period. I felt relief and, weirdly, a sense of pride.

I was just glad to have crossed this important bridge and crossed it while I was still in eighth grade. I'd go into the summer and into high school as a fully functioning, grown-up girl.

But then there was the stain. Ugh. The Pink Locker Society had counseled at least ten girls on this very problem. I wiped up as best I could. There wasn't a lot of blood. It's just that what was there had gone unattended too long. I tried to look at my backside to see how much of the stain was visible to the casual observer. It was hard to tell because the bathroom was so tiny and cramped. I couldn't get a good view. I washed my hands and looked at myself in the mirror. My shirt was too short to pull down over the stain. And I had no sweater (packed in the cargo hold!) to wrap around my waist. I sighed over my inability to use the oldest and most-often-recommended trick in the book. I also sighed that I had no period supplies with me. I had left them back at home with my soda tab bracelet and my straightening iron.

I knew I couldn't stay in there forever. It was a little too much like hiding inside my locker. I had to get out of there, but not all the way back to my seat. Taylor! She was a girl. She was closer than my own seat. And she had even asked me to stop by. It would look totally normal. I moved briskly to where she was sitting and then, oddly, squatted down, gripping her arm rest for support.

"Jemma, there you are," Taylor said.

She was sitting with Tia, whose white earphones dangled from her ears. I was grateful for the semi-privacy.

"Um, do you have any, you know, pads?" I whispered.

"Yeah, I think so," she said, and started digging through her stylish silver purse.

"What do ya need?" Tia said, pulling her earphones out. "I have gum."

"She doesn't need gum," Taylor said. "It's that time of the month."

"Oh! I have one. I'm sure of it," and she also started rooting through her bag.

"What's everyone searching for?" Luke said. "Cause I'm right here."

"Uh, Luke, hello. We're looking for-for . . . gum! And I just found it. Gum. Who doesn't love gum?" Taylor said.

I just sat in my crouched position, praying for him to move along.

"Want some gum, Luke?" I asked.

"Nah, we're eating bagels up front."

And with that, he left. Taylor reached her hand

deep into her purse, like it was a magician's hat, and pulled out a P-A-D.

"Thank you!" I whispered. I grabbed it and held it in my closed fist.

"Here's my sweatshirt," Taylor said. "In case there's stainage."

"Yes, thank you," I said, "so much."

I reached around my crouching self and tied Taylor's gray hoodie at my waist. Then I made the short trip back to the still-vacant restroom.

I peeled the strips of paper from the pad's adhesive strips and pressed it in place. No one tells you which side goes up, which is a little confusing. But I figured either way it would do the job. I washed up again and, much relieved, headed back to my seat. But first I stopped to talk to Taylor.

"All good now?"

"Much better, thanks," I said. "Hey, I never even asked you about Clem."

To the annoyance of all, Clem claimed to be an expert on New York due to all her modeling shoots there.

"It was okay," Taylor said. "She was too busy giving directions to the bus driver."

"That is so her," I said. "Well, I'm glad you came."

Then we both started laughing because we were thinking about the one very practical reason why I was glad Taylor was there, on the bus, with supplies in her purse.

Back at my seat, I decided not to share my big news. I felt fine, but the situation felt new and shaky. I just wanted to sit still and get home, keeping the shock to myself. Which brings up another point: Just because the Pink Locker Society answers girls' questions about puberty and stuff doesn't mean we think that everyone has to be blabbing all the time about this stuff. It's private, and it felt especially private to me at that moment. Of course I told Kate, but not until days later when my jeans were once again clean and Taylor's sweatshirt had been washed and returned.

But I did have something to share when I finally snaked my way back to my seat.

"I think I have our third nominee for next year's Pink Locker Society," I said. "Taylor Mayweather."

Thirty-four

No one would have admitted it, but it felt good to see our town and have the bus lurch into the school parking lot. Everyone's parents were waiting. Some sat in their cars. Others leaned against minivans, chatting. My mother was easy to spot as she was even more ginormously pregnant than she was when I left.

"Why didn't you send Dad?" I asked with concern, the first words tumbling out of my mouth.

"It's good to see you, too," she said sarcastically, and shimmied back into the driver's seat. "Well, I wanted to see you. I missed you," she said. "And I've been bored senseless at home with nothing to do."

"How are you feeling?"

"Well, they say the babies dropped, which is a good sign."

"How can that be good?"

"It just means they're lower, ready for the big day. Enough about me. How was your trip?"

"Good. Fun. Fast," I said.

"And your presentation went well? Your principal already posted a photo from the event on the school's Web site," she said.

"I think it went well. It just flew by. I don't even remember what I said."

"And now graduation, just two days away. This is quite a week."

"One kind of big thing did happen on the trip," I said.

"What? Something bad?"

"No. I, um, got my period."

"Oh, Jemma! How wonderful. What happened? Did you have your stuff?"

I explained that no, I didn't, and that there were some urgent laundry matters I needed to attend to. Mom listened, offered plentiful advice, and then started to gush.

"You know, I was just chatting with some of my poetry friends, and one of them had a party for her daughter when she got her first period. It's a real milestone, you know."

"Do not, under any circumstances, have a party for me. No party!"

"Okay. Okay. I guess it's a little overboard."

"It's a lot overboard," I said.

After a shower, it felt even better to be home. I felt grown-up but a little uncomfortable wearing the pad. I'd get used to it, Mom said. I sat on the bed and popped open the pink laptop to check on the PLS questions that had stacked up while we were in New York. How could we pick a stopping point when girls had questions all the time? I called both Kate and Piper with a proposal. We shouldn't pick a date to stop running the Web site, I said. We should simply keep it running over the summer and help the new girls take over and get accustomed to their new job.

"Problems don't take the summer off," I said. And I started to think about all the summer questions I had now because I had started my you-know-what.

Kate agreed. "In fact, there are a bunch of summer problems—some questions that only come up in summer," she said.

We ticked off bathing suit issues, family vacation issues, boredom issues, summer camp issues, "I haven't seen my crush in months" issues. The list went on.

"And don't forget that the new girls need to learn about how to climb into the Pink Locker Society offices and everything," Piper said.

We thought maybe Ms. Russo or Mrs. Percy could help us get into the school over the summer. Then we could show them how to do it.

"Funny how we did all this without anyone to show us, just a note," Kate said.

"We did," I said. It was only then that it hit me. What we accomplished in just one school year had been impressive, worthy of an award, even.

With our summer transition plan in place, we also agreed that Principal F. could introduce us at the graduation ceremony. With graduation less than forty-eight hours away, the clock was ticking on our pink secret.

Thirty-five

hy are graduation days always so devilishly hot? It's not like I've been to twenty graduations, but I'd been to a few. And all were stiflingly hot. Ours would be no different. Suddenly, the temperature spiked from late-spring lovely to ninety humid degrees, just in time for our outdoor graduation ceremony. We'd be wearing—what else?—heat-insulating, full-length graduation robes and caps. And my mother, as you might imagine, was a concern. No one wants a very pregnant woman standing out in sweltering heat. But she wouldn't skip it.

"Oh, no. I'm going," she said. "You'll only graduate from middle school one time and I'll be there."

When we arrived at school, Dad followed her

around like her athletic trainer, prepared with a towel, sunscreen, and cold drinks. He was also ready to whisk her inside the school building, where it was deliciously air-conditioned. I broke away to find my group. Mrs. Percy was in charge of our graduation caps. Armed with a pocket full of hairpins, she showed everyone how to wear those strange mortarboard hats with the blue tassels. When she got to me, Mrs. Percy stopped and said my cap was in a different box. She returned with a white graduation cap that had not a blue tassel, but a pink one.

"We had these made up special," she said.

"I love it," I said.

With everyone in place—from A to Z—we filed onto the athletic field and found our seats. Every spectator who was a parent was either snapping photos or taking video. I saw my parents and they waved.

"Welcome, everyone, to the hottest event in town," Principal Finklestein said to a smattering of polite laughter.

But every eighth-grader cheered when he added, "Due to the heat, I've decided to keep my remarks brief today."

I scanned the crowd for Kate and Piper who were seated with the N–Q group. I was ready, but not ready, for our big moment. Word had leaked out a bit after New York. Some people knew about Tomorrow's

Leaders Today, and some knew that the three of us were in the Pink Locker Society. But to most people, it was all still at the rumor level.

"Just stride across the stage like you own the place," Piper had told me.

"I'm just going to try not to trip," I said.

After the academic awards and the athletic awards, it was our turn. Principal F. called us by name to the stage.

"Kate Parker.

"Piper Pinsky.

"Jemma Colwin.

"It's my pleasure to introduce, for the first time, this year's Pink Locker Society," he said.

We all made it to the stage. I didn't trip. And people clapped—a good, long stretch of applause. I think my mother might have woo-hooed.

"We couldn't be prouder to have this fine organization at our school," Principal Finklestein said. "It was recently recognized as a national model at the Tomorrow's Leaders Today conference."

The audience, weary from the heat, gave another smattering of applause. We stood on the stage, ready to be dismissed from view.

"Oh, and I have one more announcement," Principal F. said. "The Pink Locker Society made such an impression at the conference that Tomorrow's

Leaders Today has invited these three girls to its international conference this July."

More applause, this time a little more spirited, erupted from the crowd. I'm nearly certain I heard my mother woo-hooing that time. I felt proud that our presentation had won an award. I wondered if Forrest would get to go, too. Then Mrs. Percy approached the stage and whispered in the principal's ear.

"I just received word that the conference they'll be attending is in Paris, France."

Again, the clapping and cheering continued. For a moment, I forgot who we were and what we were doing in the middle of the athletic field. WE WERE GOING TO PARIS!

After our group hug, Mrs. Percy guided us offstage and pointed us to a few open seats. The three of us were seated right behind Clem Caritas, of all people. She spun around and said, accusingly, "OMG, Jemma. Why didn't you tell me?" I just shrugged.

"One last note on the Pink Locker Society," Principal F. said. "Next year's members have already been selected and the advice service will be continuing into the next school year. Great job, girls."

Piper sat speechless, able to do nothing but fan herself madly with her graduation program. It wasn't until much later in the evening that she started speaking French. Lots and lots of French.

Thirty-six

OK, so I wouldn't say that I never thought of Forrest on graduation day. But I am proud to say that I wasn't thinking of him nonstop, like I used to. My mind was buzzing about the PLS, our group trip to Paris, and the big graduation dance.

Since coming home from New York, Forrest hadn't texted nor had we had any major conversations. What did I expect? Or more precisely, what did I expect once I trained myself not to expect anything? I made myself a new soda tab bracelet with four new goals for the summer before high school started:

1. Keep running so that I can make the high school track team.

2. Be a great big sister. My mom was now two days away from the due date.
3. Keep in touch with Piper when we weren't at the same school anymore. ☹
4. The pink tab: Be on call whenever the Pink Locker Society needed me. Mimi, Shannon, and Taylor had gratefully accepted their new positions, especially Taylor.

I wore no boy-related goal on my wrist. It felt a little lonely sometimes, but it was good not to be striving too hard for Forrest or twisting myself in a pretzel to like someone I didn't genuinely like as a boyfriend. Bet, also boyfriendless, was always there for me in situations just like this. We resolved not to be wallflowers (again) at the graduation dance, just like we had at the Backward Dance so many months ago. Kate and Piper were both going to the dance with dates. Bet and I were, as usual, dateless.

Dad drove us back to school for the dance. On the way, we used the backseat of the car as our makeup studio, where Bet applied some of her sparkly eye shadow on my waiting lids. Dad dropped us off in front of the school, where there was a moon bounce and an outdoor dance floor. The sun had set and the temperature fell so it felt warm, but not unpleasant.

Good, I thought, I don't want all my sparkly eye shadow to melt right off.

Picnic tables were scattered around and each had a helium balloon centerpiece. Bet and I got ourselves something to drink and started to survey the crowd. The DJ was taking requests, which kept the dance floor full. But the moon bounce turned out to be the biggest draw. You wouldn't think eighth-graders would want to jump and bounce and do flips off the walls, but we did. Because the music speakers were positioned nearby, you could dance in there, too. Maybe without admitting it, we eighth-graders don't always feel like growing up and being mature. The line for the moon bounce wrapped around the dance floor and the refreshments table. And everyone was walking around barefoot because no shoes were allowed.

The moon bounce also took some of the usual dance pressure off. If we were all sweaty and jumping around like preschoolers, we didn't feel as much need to pair up. I wondered if high school students still liked moon bounces. I'm guessing if they did no one admitted it. So we bounced and bounced and, when we weren't bouncing, we were waiting in line for another turn.

"Jemma! Come in with us," Forrest called to me from near the front of the line.

Bet arched her eyebrow and said she was going to

shoot some video of the festivities. Before I could argue, she was gone.

"Do you care if I cut ahead?" I asked a group behind him, which included Clem Caritas.

Everyone said no and Clem said nothing. Typical Clem. I slid into line with Forrest.

"How's your mom?" Forrest asked.

Everyone had seen her at graduation. I mean, the woman could not be missed.

"She's okay. One more day until the due date."

"I had a really good time in New York," Forrest said. "It was beast."

"Beast. Yes, it was. I never said, but I liked your pink tie."

Forrest smiled. Luke Zubin came up behind us and put an arm around each of us.

"When are you two kids just going to get together already?"

"Luke!" I said, annoyed. I flicked his arm off my shoulder.

"Zubin, dude. Get a hold of yourself," Forrest said, but stayed in Luke's embrace.

"All I'm saying is it's like the last day of eighth grade. It's now or never, unless you're going to Charter like smarty-pants McCann here," Luke said.

"You're going to Charter, too, Luke," Forrest said.

"Okay, that's technically true," he said.

"Where are you going to high school, Jemma?" Luke asked me.

"Charter. Kate and I both got in," I said.

I watched Forrest's expression change. He looked surprised, but in a good way.

"There you go, then," Luke said. "It was meant to be. Tell her about the flower, Forrest." Before I could say, "What flower?" Luke left in the direction of the ice cream sundae bar.

"Zubin is such a bonehead," Forrest said.

"Yeah," I said.

"I'm glad, though, that you're going to Charter," Forrest said.

"It's a really good school," I said.

"I mean I'm glad you're going to be there, too," Forrest said.

"What did he mean about the flower? What flower?" I asked.

Forrest looked to the sky like he was trying to figure out what to say.

"He means the carnation sale. I . . . um . . . sent you a pink carnation."

"You sent it?"

"Well, you got more than one, I figured it would just blend in," Forrest said.

"It did not blend. It was the only pink one. And it had no note."

"Yeah, I didn't know what to say."

"Big shock," I said. "You once told me you didn't know how you felt."

"And you didn't like that answer."

"No."

"I don't always not know," Forrest said.

"Whatever that means," I said, half wanting to change the subject. "This line is taking forever."

I looked away because the intensity was starting to make my palms sweat. My phone vibrated in my skirt pocket, but I ignored it. I looked at Forrest and, for the first time, I believed he might actually like me. But to go any further felt like jumping off a ledge into the deep end. I swallowed hard.

"Say it," I said.

"Say what?" he said.

"If you like me or not."

My heart was beating really hard. My palms were slick and my phone would not stop shaking like a Chihuahua in my pocket.

"I like you, Jemma."

I took a deep breath through my nose and nodded my head. Why was I nodding? Because I agreed, or was I saying I liked him, too?

"It's our turn," Forrest said.

For a moment, I thought he was being romantic. *Finally, it's our turn!* But it actually was *our turn*. For the moon bounce. Mr. Ford was holding the flap on the moon bounce door for us.

You might think: What bad timing! But really, a moon bounce was just the right place for me to burn off the nervous energy that had accumulated in me over the last ten minutes. I bounced over to Piper and simply screamed. She screamed back, having no idea that my scream had a reason. I caught a glimpse of Bet, who was filming us from the other side of the moon bounce netting. She winked at me. I kept an eye on Forrest, who was turning some impressive flips and hockey-checking his friends against the moon bounce walls. Then Mr. Ford blew his whistle and our turn was up.

I went looking for my shoes and wondered if Forrest would just drift off, like the last fifteen minutes had been a dream. But as I slipped on my ballet flats, he appeared beside me. People were swirling around us, finding their shoes, taking shoes off, snapping photos, heading to and from the dance floor. Forrest looked down at the ground and took my hand. When I looked down at my hand's new location, he stepped a foot closer and kissed me. It was soft and quick, almost secretive. My feet felt frozen in place. I just stood and looked at him.

Why did he like me now? How long would it last? I wanted to know what had changed. And I didn't want to be hurt if he ever stopped liking me. But I knew in my bones that I would not get answers to my questions. Why? Because people were complicated and you couldn't really know what was going on inside someone's heart. You were lucky enough to understand your own.

Brrrttt! Brrrttt!

My phone! I had been ignoring it basically forever. I looked at the screen and saw it was my dad.

"Jemma? Finally. Your mom is in labor and we're at the hospital. She's fine, but you'll need to get a ride home."

"What? You mean it's happening tonight?"

"Yes, probably. But sometimes these things take a while. Mrs. Pinsky can take you home," he said.

"She's okay? Mom is, right?"

"Of course—this isn't her first time doing this, you know," Dad said.

"Tell her I love her," I said.

"You've got it," Dad said excitedly.

I ended the call and was closer to crying than I wanted to be.

"Is everything okay?" Forrest asked, still holding my hand.

"No . . . yes . . . I think. My mom is having the baby. The babies!"

"Do you have to go?" he asked.

"I think I do."

I reached out and hugged him.

"Let me know, as soon as you know," he said.

"Done," I said.

I spun around, a woman with a plan. Why should I just hang here like nothing was happening? I should *be there*. This was big—was it not? I found Bet and Kate, and finally, Piper. Mrs. Pinsky agreed to pick us up, but she was reluctant to let all of us go to the hospital.

"You're going to have to ask the front desk nurse if it's okay that you're all there. It's a hospital, for goodness' sakes," she said.

We said our quick good-byes to the rest of our friends. Piper stopped briefly, like a celebrity, to sign someone's yearbook before dashing off to her mom's car.

"Are you sure this is okay?" Mrs. Pinsky asked. "I'm sure your mother doesn't want an audience."

"We're not going into the delivery room," I said. "We can play cards or something."

The thought of watching a baby being born filled me with fear, actually. Childbirth was thrilling, mysterious, and terrifying. How did something so miraculous happen every single day everywhere on the planet?

The wide glass hospital doors slid open and we

got directions to the maternity wing. A soothing peach waiting room, nearly empty, awaited us. I told the nurse I wanted to see my dad and, in a few moments, he appeared.

"Jemma, what are you doing here? What are you all doing here?"

"I wanted to come. And I'm old enough. We can just wait together, right?"

"Well, okay. Things are moving right along actually," he said. "Do you want to come in and see your mom?"

"I can do that?"

"Of course, she's in a nice, private room."

My dad and I walked down a corridor past rooms where little plastic cribs sat next to each hospital bed. Balloons and flowers announced whether it was a girl or boy. I heard a few baby cries, but they weren't that loud. I started to wonder if maybe babies didn't start to cry in that loud, wake-you-up way until they were a little older. Mom's room was cozy despite all the bleeping and blipping medical monitoring equipment. She looked OK to me.

"Hi, Mom."

"How are you, cupcake? How was the dance?"

"It was good. Really good. But I'm glad I'm here now."

"Me, too. Do you want to stay?"

"You mean stay, *stay*? As in be here when the babies are born?"

"Shouldn't we have talked about that before?" Dad interrupted. "This is kind of sudden for her."

"I just thought of it now," Mom said. "But only if you want to."

I did and I didn't, but I did. I raced out to the waiting room to tell my BFFs. Then I raced back into the delivery room, where the doctors and nurses were focused, like laser beams, on the babies. How were their hearts beating? What position were they in? I did not like seeing my mother in any kind of pain, but she told me she could do it. She worked extremely hard—like someone running a marathon—and we couldn't do much to help, except be cheerleaders. Dad and I held her hands. We made jokes and I prayed feverishly that everyone would be OK. Then, gloriously, the babies emerged from the watery inside world to the airy world out here with us.

"It's a girl," the smiling doctor said.

An umbilical cord was cut and I heard a sweet cry. I wanted so much to hold her right then, but she needed to be checked out and weighed first.

"It's . . . another girl," the still-smiling doctor said.

Another cord was cut. Another cry was heard. Mom was OK. I cried tears of happiness and I think Dad cried a little, too.

"How long until we can see them?" I asked my dad.

"You can see them right now," a nurse said.

She handed one blanketed baby to me and another to my dad.

"Stand by your mom and smile," said a nurse holding a camera. "Cheese!"

A flash went off and the printer started printing our first family portrait.

"Is everyone good?" Mom asked.

"They're perfect," said the doctor. "Congratulations."

"Jemma, sit on the edge of the bed there with your mom so I can take another picture," Dad said.

I sat down carefully with one sister in my arms. He handed me one more. I smiled down at them. I had held little babies before, but not this new. They were red-faced and warm as toast, two little pink-blanket burritos. In a minute, I would rush out to the waiting room and share the news with Kate, Piper, and Bet. And I had promised to text Forrest. But I didn't want to let them go, or let go of this moment, just yet.

Now that we knew they were not boys, I could admit that I was hoping for sisters all along. My parents had kept the names totally top-secret, even from me, for fear that someone wouldn't like one of the choices.

But I loved the names they chose. I fast-forwarded the memories I wanted to share with my baby sisters: first steps and playgrounds, Christmas mornings and first days of school.

Years from now, I would tell them about the Pink Locker Society, too. When they are in middle school, I'll be twenty-four—amazingly old. Because they're my sisters, they could be legacy members, a gift handed down through time. But I was getting ahead of myself. And I knew I should be going. My friends had been waiting forever for my wonderful news. I kissed the top of each tiny head and silently welcomed them, Ivy and Rose, the newest links in our pink chain.

Ask the PLS

How do we answer over 30,000 questions?

That's how many questions have been sent in to the Pink Locker Society Web site. But here's the good news: Girls often have the same or very similar questions. Here are some of the most popular ones.

What are the signs I will get my period soon?
Certain signs give you a hint that your first period will arrive soon. But these signs aren't the kind of thing that will let you predict the exact day and time. Use them as guidelines.

A first period usually happens:

- between ages ten and fifteen
- about two to two and a half years after a girl begins developing breasts
- after about six months of getting vaginal discharge, a thick, white mucus (most girls notice it in their underwear)

If you're concerned that your first period will surprise you, be prepared and carry a couple of pads with you. Lots of girls stash them in a pencil case in their backpacks, just in case.

I need a bigger bra, but I'm afraid to tell my mom. What do I do?
Breasts grow gradually, so it's totally normal to grow out of your bra. Girls seem to stress a little over asking their moms to go bra shopping. Why? Probably because they are a little uncomfortable talking to their moms about personal, puberty stuff.

So we understand it's a little awkward, but usually not as bad as wearing a too-tight bra. Pick a time when you're alone with your mom and just ask plainly, "Mom, my bra is tight. Can we look for a new one?" Some girls find it's easier to ask when you're at a store and you are walking near the bra department. Before you know it, you'll be in a new, more comfortable, and supportive bra.

How do I know if a boy likes me?

Sigh. I wish we had the answer to this one. It turns out the answer is lots of different answers. That's according to all the girls who offered their advice on the Pink Locker Society blog. Here are some of them:

- He looks at you a lot
- He won't look at you
- He smiles at you
- He tries to make you laugh
- He is mean to you
- He blushes when he talks to you
- He talks to you
- He won't talk to you

Are you confused? We are, too!

I'm jealous of my friend who's prettier/smarter/ more popular than me. How can I compete with her?

We've all been there. You have this friend who's funny and wonderful and beautiful. It's just that sometimes her wonderfulness makes you feel less so. She's the life of the party and everyone wants to sit next to her at lunch. What can you do?

1. Don't get angry with her. Very likely she's just being herself, not trying to make you feel bad.
2. Focus on your strengths. We are sure you have great qualities and talents. Work on stuff that you enjoy, whether it's music or sports or bird-watching. You'll feel less jealous—and happier—if you're following your own path.
3. Be honest with her, in a kind way. If you feel left out, it's OK to say so. People don't always notice when a friend's feelings are hurt. It's fine to ask her to be more sensitive, but remember that the solution to the jealousy problem is you!

How can I get a question answered on the Pink Locker Society blog?

We receive A LOT of questions, but you always have a chance! Go to pinklockersociety.org and submit your question on the Ask the PLS page.

It's located here: www.pinklockersociety.org/ask/ask.html.

On that page, you'll also find a bunch of already-answered questions, including these:

• What can you do if your boobs are too big?
• I'm the tallest girl in my class. Will I ever stop growing?
• Do periods hurt?

After submitting your question, check the PLS blog page to see if it gets answered.

It's here: blog.pinklockersociety.org.

And while you're there, please give the Pink Locker world some of your fabulous advice!

Spread the Kindness!

In *Girls in Charge*, Jemma helps Taylor deal with a bully even though Jemma isn't exactly Taylor's BFF.

If you see someone being bullied, tell a grown-up. Even better, consider escorting the person away from the situation. Just say "Come on. Let's go." All of a sudden, the bully is alone without a victim. And you have done a good deed.

These Web sites offer good ideas about how to reduce bullying. Check them out!

Kind Campaign
Finding Kind is a movie and a movement. Two twenty-something women traveled across the United States to interview girls about meanness and bullying. Now

the filmmaker duo wants girls everywhere to take a pledge to be nicer.

www.kindcampaign.com

Brigitte Berman

High school student Brigitte Berman became an anti-bullying advocate to help other young people. Brigitte, once a bullying victim herself, wrote a bullying survival guide and often takes her show on the road and visits with school groups.

www.doriewitt.com

Stop Bullying

This federal government site offers specialized advice for kids, teens, and even adults. The bottom line: Don't suffer in silence.

www.stopbullying.gov

Be Strong, Girls!

The Pink Locker Society characters are each strong in their own ways. But what is strength? You can be physically strong, like when you're fit and healthy. You can also show you're strong when you do something challenging, like running a race.

It takes a strong girl to do what's right, like when Jemma helped Taylor with her bullying situation. And you can gain strength when you learn how to take charge and become a leader.

Want to be a strong girl and someday a strong woman? These groups can show you how it's done!

Best Bones Forever
Let's start with physical strength and health. What you do (and eat) when you're young affects how strong your bones will be for your whole life. Did you know that dancing is good for your bones?

www.bestbonesforever.gov

Girl Scouts
Being a Girl Scout means a lot more than selling cookies. Through fun activities, the program builds confidence and inspires girls to think like leaders.

www.girlscouts.org/forgirls

Girls on the Run
Like Jemma, thousands of girls start running every year. Girls on the Run helps girls train to run a 5K race (about three miles). Think you can't possibly run that far? Oh, yes you can!

www.girlsontherun.org

Did you know...
Friendship can help solve bullying.
Find out more at:
KidsHealth.org/friends
The #1 most-visited site about health and development for kids and teens
KidsHealth
from Nemours

Viva La Pink Locker Society!

Book 1

Book 2

Book 3

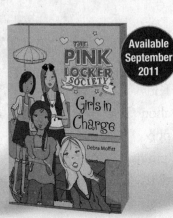

Book 4

Visit **www.PinkLockerSociety.org** to read excerpts, play games, and ask your own questions of Jemma and the rest of the PLS!

 www.facebook.com/pinklockersociety

ST. MARTIN'S GRIFFIN

Tarquin Cardona

About the Author

Debra Moffitt lives in a house full of boys—with three sons and one husband. She was a newspaper reporter for more than ten years and is now the kids' editor of KidsHealth.org. That means she gets paid to write about stuff kids care about, like pimples, crushes, and puberty. She'd like to thank all the girls who visit www.pinklockersociety.org. You've asked over 30,000 questions about growing up and have given tons of kind, thoughtful advice to one another. That's thinking pink!